Hidden Dreams

BINDARRA CREEK CHRISTMAS IN JULY ROMANCE

SUZANNE GILCHRIST

MALLEE STAR ENTERPRISES

Hidden Dreams

Bindarra Creek Christmas in July Romance

By

SUZANNE GILCHRIST

Other books by the author

Writing as: SUZANNE GILCHRIST
Sweet, small town romances

Cowboy under the Mistletoe (Edge of the Outback Romance)
Dance in the Outback (Edge of the Outback Romance)
The Cowboy's Gift (Edge of the Outback Romance)
Under an Outback Sky (Edge of the Outback Romance)

Bindarra Creek Makeover (A Bindarra Creek Romance)
Love's Sweet Challenge (Bindarra Creek Short & Sweet Romance)
Take Me Home (Bindarra Creek A Town Reborn)
A Dangerous Secret (Bindarra Creek Mystery Romance)
The Mistletoe Wish (Bindarra Creek Christmas Romance)

The Glitter or the Gold (Bindarra Creek Small Town Christmas)
Hidden Dreams (Bindarra Creek Christmas in July)

A Life with You (Outback Hearts)
Only You (Outback Hearts) – coming late 2025

Writing as: S. E. GILCHRIST
SCIENCE FICTION / SPACE OPERA / POST APOCALYPTIC

Darkon Warriors Spicy alien romance series:
Legend Beyond the Stars
The Portal
Awakening the Warriors
Star Pirate's Justice
When Stars Collide
Bargain with the Enemy
Touring the Stars
The Slave Trap

Post-Apocalyptic Spicy romances:
Paying the Forfeit
Storm of Fire
Quest for Earth

Sci Fi / Space Exploration romance series:
Stranded (Mars Academy)
Cosmic Fire (Mars Academy)

New Adult Apocalyptic books:
Don't Look Back (Warders of Earth)

CONTEMPORARY SPICY ROMANTIC SUSPENSE

Scent of the Jaguar (Deadly Forces novel)

FANTASY/ANCIENT WORLDS EROTIC ROMANCE

Bound by Love
Bound by Lies

HIDDEN DREAMS

Copyright © 2025 Suzanne Gilchrist
ISBN: 978-1-7641019-0-5

Dedication

For all those who dream of second chances.

Author's Website: www.segilchrist.com

Bindarra Creek Romances

Drama, intrigue, suspense, adventure and honest, country goodness – welcome to Bindarra Creek where life and love in a small country town has never been more challenging.

Books in the Bindarra Creek universe by the Author:

Bindarra Creek Makeover
Love's Sweet Challenge
Take Me Home
A Dangerous Secret
The Mistletoe Wish
The Glitter or The Gold
Hidden Dreams

Chapter One

"A Christmas in July?" Pixie Wellington stared at her brother with mounting excitement as they parked up outside the small building that used to be Fig Tree Lodge's old stables before her family renovated it into self-contained quarters. She exited the car, and began to tug her bags from the trunk, her chest tightening when Kirk joined her with a happy grin. She couldn't believe how much she had missed the big galoot.

Nodding, Kirk grabbed her largest suitcase, then a slightly smaller one, propelling them in front of him, while prodding her back with his elbow, urging her into motion.

"Yep. Business has been a bit slow since January, so

the other night, the Country Women's Association brainstormed a plan to draw tourists back into the town."

A brisk wind sent fallen leaves tumbling along the gravel drive, rich with the citrusy scent of an old lemon tree growing nearby. Pixie filled her lungs with all that good country freshness and gave a happy skip.

"This will be perfect for me. The festival idea and your wedding are exactly what I need to take my business to the next level."

Pixie did her best to deflect her brother's suddenly suspicious glance with a limpid expression. She knew what her track record was like where work was concerned, one her family had grown all too familiar with over the years. But Kirk's announcement had to be an omen that both luck and her life were about to take a turn for the better - and she didn't intend to waste the opportunity.

"Now, Pix..."

Giving an airy toss of her head, she interrupted before he could reach full flow and start one of his big brother lectures he was so fond of giving.

"I'll go for a walk after I've said my hellos to everyone and begin posting the news immediately on my sites. Think of it as free advertising."

He frowned. "Aren't your followers based in America? What we need is a promotional pitch aimed at the Aussie market."

"Bro, leave it with me. This is what I excel at." Pixie

heaved her other large case over a rut in the drive, panting slightly with the effort since the bag weighed a tonne. "What does the committee have in mind?"

"Quite a lot. I can't believe how fast they have moved, given the idea was only broached a few days ago at their last meeting." He shook his head, smiling.

"That will be our cousin Edwina's doing. She sure is some powerhouse of a lady."

They shared a fond grin. It had taken a mere sixty seconds for their first cousin, once removed, to become firmly entrenched in their hearts, along with Edwina's grandson Dodge, his wife Tessa and their two daughters Kaylee and Tilly. Not to mention the rest of the extended family – along with their friends. Come to think of it, maybe that was the entire town?

"I'm not sure about using your influencer platforms ..." began Kirk.

"It'll be fine," Pixie cut in, her voice sharp and her glance narrow as she glared, causing him to clamp his mouth shut on what would no doubt be more objections.

She wailed as one of the wheels came off her bag, and it crunched to the ground.

"Why did you park so far from the front door?"

The bulging backpack, which contained her precious laptop and which she had slung over one shoulder, slipped down her arm, and she caught it just in time before it too could tumble to the ground.

"Hey, I parked where it suited me best. Remember I told you I'm living in the converted stables now?"

His easy tone told her he had decided not to pursue the topic, but she wasn't fooled. She knew her brother; he'd be back on it like a dog with a bone the instant he thought the moment was right. But that was okay. It gave her more time to come up with opposing arguments about his possible concerns.

"I guess." Twisting around, she glanced back for a brief moment at where the brick and iron-roofed building nestled between a copse of shady trees. The newly added narrow porch, where a couple of comfy cane chairs and several potted plants were situated, ran the full length of the front of the small dwelling and gave off a cosy, welcoming vibe.

She heaved her case over the rough ground as they rounded the corner of the main building and approached the front entrance. "It doesn't look like you have a lot of room, though. Where do you fit all your stuff?"

"It's big enough for me and Billie. I've got a few possessions that I rarely use packed away in the local storage sheds. We're looking for a place to buy but haven't seen anything that ticks all our boxes yet."

"Are you still studying to be a teacher?"

"Sure am, one and half years to go. I board at a bedsit during the week in Tamworth, where the college is situated, and try to make it home as much as possible."

"Once upon a time, home was the States." She shot him a careful look.

Kirk shrugged. "What can I say? This town called to me."

"And there's Billie."

"I won't deny she is the major factor behind my staying here. Hey, you look like you're struggling a bit. Give me that case, and you take this small one."

"Thanks a bunch."

As they came closer, her gaze travelled over Fig Tree Lodge, the historic building that had been the Lette family home for well over a century and lingered on the massive tree that dominated the enormous front yard, as if on centre stage of a theatre production. A tyre swing hung from a low-lying branch; the shade engendered by the ancient tree dark and cool and where stunning purple flowers bloomed at the base of its thick trunk.

Pixie recalled how enraptured she had felt the moment she had set eyes on the Lodge nearly two years ago, the first time she had visited Australia. And the first time she had connected with relatives she had previously known by name only. She had enjoyed herself so much she had extended her holiday for longer than initially anticipated, surprised at the sense of home she had encountered. This visit would be her second, and she sensed it wouldn't disappoint. That dizzy feeling she was poised on the edge of something wonderful refused to budge no matter how hard she attempted to reason with herself with cold, hard logic. And now, with Kirk's news about the event the town was planning, she had difficulty in tamping down her rampant anticipation.

"I see the place has had a fresh coat of paint. It's looking good."

"Sure is; Dodge has almost completed all the necessary renovations to bring the old girl back to her glory days. I've been giving him a hand where I can." Kirk affected a modest smirk that utterly failed to convince Pixie.

She snorted. "As if. You wouldn't know one end of a hammer if it hit you on the head."

"Cheeky!" Kirk shoulder nudged her.

Chuckling, she skipped ahead, her eagerness to see everyone again firing up her energy that had flagged after the long flight from LA.

"Seriously, I'm glad you came, sis." His voice was sober.

She turned her head to look at him. "You're really going through with it?"

"I sure am – and looking forward to the next chapter of my life. With Billie. Speaking of whom, there she is." Kirk bounded up the steps, eyes fixed on where Billie waited, a big smile lighting up her face.

"Wow. You don't travel light, do you? How long are you staying again?"

Then she chuckled to take any perceived sting from her words, running down the few steps to hug Pixie.

"Great to see you again. And thanks so much for agreeing to be part of the bridal party."

After they pulled apart, Billie took charge of one of

the suitcases and easily heaved it onto the wide front porch that circumnavigated the entire house.

"What choice do I have? My big brother doesn't get married any old day. However, I find it weird that I will be the best man. Or rather the best woman?" Dropping the bags' handles, Pixie struck a *'Rocky'* pose, causing Billie and Kirk to grin.

Billie winked. "Wait until you meet the chief bridesman."

"This sure is going to be a ceremony to remember. But I know it will be awesome. By the way, I intend to post some of the wedding footage to my social media accounts."

Pushing open the main door, Billie raised her eyebrows.

"Did I miss something?"

"Pixie has been telling me about her new business."

"More of a career," Pixie said firmly. "I've got over fifteen thousand followers, and my numbers are growing daily. It won't be long, and I'll be a household name. Which reminds me, I must do a post."

She stopped in the foyer, slipped her backpack around to her front and rummaged inside. A second later, she was fixing her mobile phone to a selfie stick and fluffing up her short hair.

"How do I look? Not too worn out after the flight?"

Her belly fluttered at that thought, and she turned anxiously towards Billie, who looked more than a little bemused but also shook her head in a friendly fashion.

"You look lovely. You always do," said Billie.

Pixie focussed on the tiny camera window and puffed out a long breath to steady her voice before beginning to record.

"Well, here I am, folks. After a seventeen-hour flight and a six-hour train ride from Sydney, I finally arrived in Tamworth, where my gorgeous bro waited at the station. Check him out, peeps."

One swift motion and she turned the camera to Kirk, grimacing inwardly at his startled rabbit expression. Gathering himself, he flashed a charming smile so reminiscent of his previous persona of an up-and-coming Hollywood star that Pixie felt quite misty inside, her chest swelling with pride.

"You may remember him as the star in the popular daytime soap *Law, Love and Loss*. Now, he's settled down in a small country town and ... wait for it ..."

She trilled an infectious peel of laughter.

"Is getting hitched. Very soon. But that's enough for today. More coming soon."

She winked at the camera and then turned off the recording.

"How did that sound? Natural enough? My catchwords are ethical consumerism and authenticity; and so far, it's proving a real winner."

"I'm no expert with social media, but I think you nailed it," said Billie.

"Perfect."

Humming, Pixie began videoing the foyer, giving the wide wooden staircase and chandelier lengthy play time.

"Maybe check with Auntie Edwina before you post anything about Fig Tree Lodge."

"You think?" Pixie stared at Billie for a couple of beats before shrugging. "If you say so."

"It's the polite thing to do," interposed Kirk as he trundled the last of her cases inside and then pulled the door to.

Pixie made a moue with her lips, then rolled her eyes.

"Even though this place also belongs to us Wellingtons, I'll play ball. But I want footage of your wedding."

After sharing a glance with Billie, Kirk threw his hands in the air. "Only after we've vetted what you want to share."

"Deal." Pixie picked up her backpack, ensuring her brother couldn't spot how she had crossed her fingers.

"Am I in the same room as last time? I need a hot shower and a change of clothes before seeing anyone else."

"Stinky some." Kirk grinned and hoisted a bag under each arm as he began to climb the stairs.

She snorted. "Nice! Not."

Half an hour later, Pixie was a new woman. Recording as she went, she went downstairs to the kitchen, remembering how everyone liked to gather there in the late afternoon while Dodge prepared the meals. He was the Lodge's official chief; however, she understood from conversations with her brother, that whenever Dodge's father and stepmom were in residence, they took over the kitchen.

Ignoring Billie's suggestion to check with Edwina first, she had already uploaded another two posts onto her sites. The first one was where she shared her delight in the room, hers for the duration of her stay and decorated with an ancient Egyptian theme. Edwina or Tessa had chosen rich, earthy browns, royal blues and gold colours to create the effect of opulence. A deep blue chaise with gold brocade cushions, made a stunning focal point. Gauzy cream fabric that fell to the floor in luscious folds draped the old-fashioned four-poster bed; the bedspread was a mosaic of browns, tans and white and contrasted with dramatic effect with white beaded cushions. A magnificent wall tapestry hung on one wall depicting the pyramids at sunset. There were ornately framed prints and several statues of some old Egyptian gods such as Anubis, Isis, and Bastet (the only ones Pixie recognised from her brief one-year stint at college when she had fancied herself as an archaeologist). The curtains framing the twin set of French doors that opened to the veranda were similar to the fabric draping the dark timbered bed frame.

Her second post had been of the view from the upstairs veranda, which she had to admit had stolen her breath for a few seconds. She had leaned on the balustrade, gazing out at the extensive grounds of Fig Tree Lodge and enjoying the kiss of a cold wind as it vanquished the last of her travel fatigue. The scent of country mixed with lemon teased her nostrils and stirred up a confusing mix of emotions as she soaked up the ambience. There was no sound of traffic only birdsong and the distant shouts of some kids goofing off, and the tension of the past day bled from her stiff bones. It was so peaceful here and felt like home in some strange fashion. The setting sun had gilded the leaves in a nearby tree with oranges and reds, glowing as if on fire as the rays highlighted the differing hues of early fall.

No, that wasn't right. Aussies called this time of year autumn; she made a mental note to mention that snippet in her next clip. She thought it would strike exactly the right note with the *tone* she wanted to convey: fun, inspirational, and with a teasing educational fragment. Not too much, though; who wanted to know stuff anyway?

Running her free hand over the smooth surface of the banister, she all but floated down the stairs and along the hall following the rise and fall of voices. The knowledge that she had already uploaded two additional videos without running them past Edwina was all but forgotten. There had been nothing in them surely that could give rise to any concern. Kirk had always been an old fuddy-duddy, a stickler for the rules. While Pixie thought of rules as – guidelines.

Grinning as another famous line from one of her fav movies ran through her head, she danced into the kitchen.

"I'm back," she called out.

Her brain fizzed and snapped with ideas on how she'd weave the wedding and an Aussie Christmas in July into posts that would catapult her to the mega status she craved.

This was the break she had been waiting for; and the future she'd yearned for so long was right around the corner.

Chapter Two

He never should have come.

He never should have agreed to be Billie's male bridesmaid or whatever the correct terminology was.

And he definitely never should have accepted a dinner invitation at Fig Tree Lodge. Not with Billie's fiancée sitting directly opposite and him having to witness every loving glance they shared.

Not with Ms Edwina Lette's infamous far-too-seeing eagle eyes glued to his face.

Jordan fought the urge to squirm, his arm bumping the American woman's hand when he reached for his glass of wine, causing her to drop her mobile phone.

Thinking about his dinner partner triggered another point of contention, which had begun to eat away at him

13

the moment he entered the dining room and they had been introduced; she with a camera right up in his face like she was some kind of Hollywood movie producer.

Who in their right mind recorded themselves eating?

Why on earth didn't someone say something about it, anyway?

Shaking his head, he snuck a sideways glance at her as she hummed under her breath and propped the phone back up against the saltshaker.

"What do you think?" She gestured at her half-eaten meal of roast pork and roasted vegetables all but obscured under a sea of rich gravy.

"Huh?"

Think about what?

The food?

The cutlery?

The current price of wool?

What?

Mind blank, he stared at her. He knew he'd become a bit of a hermit these past few years, mainly where women were concerned, but that didn't explain the crazy, panicked feeling that came over him when faced with bright, iridescent green eyes that seemed to dance as he sat, plopped in his seat, like a sack of potatoes. He could feel the energy charging from her with enough voltage to power up half the state and wondered how soon he could decently escape.

Ms Lette suddenly let loose with a cackle that sent icy shivers prickling up and down his spine and hot sweat dampening his armpits. Her witchy chortle had captured everyone's attention - everyone equating to way too many people (in Jordan's point of view) since the room overflowed with her and Billie's relatives, as well as the militant Mrs Brown, who had struck fear into him at the age of three (and which he had never quite overcome) and the elderly, charming Fukuka's. Even Billie's dad, Mr Miller, was in attendance, although his dazed expression told the story of someone who didn't know where he was and maybe wasn't sure who he was either. A pang of sadness spasmed through Jordan, remembering the kindly man who'd drifted in and out of the days of his childhood. If Jordan's mother had the gossip correct, the poor bloke had been diagnosed with dementia a few years ago. Pastor Miller, Billie's mum, edged a glass of water into her husband's hand and gave him an encouraging nod.

Jordan dragged his mind back to his present dilemma.

Ms Lette was looking at him. The Yankee woman was looking at him. Damn, everyone was looking at him.

He winced under the barrage of eyes.

Not good.

Not good at all.

Maybe he could drop his knife and spend the remainder of the dinner under the table pretending to look for it.

Before he had to resort to such measures, Billie, his

sweet Billie or the woman who used to be his sweet Billie, came to the rescue.

Just like she always had done.

"I'd appreciate it if you put the phone away now, Pixie."

Pixie. What kind of name was that?

"I'm right on it."

A few clicks with polished red nails that looked sharp and long enough to rip a man's throat wide open, and a second later, the phone was lying on the table.

Hoping the anxious beads of sweat lining his forehead didn't show, Jordan gulped wine and gazed across at the woman who had been his best mate since kindergarten.

The woman who, at the age of sixteen, he'd thought would be his wife.

The woman who, at eighteen, fled their small hometown and rarely returned during the past twenty-three years - until, that is, just over two years ago. As always, the sight of Billie's familiar face loosened the old familiar knot of nerves in his gut. Despite the years, she didn't look very different from the memory of her he'd hidden deep in his heart.

"Well? You didn't answer my question?"

The voice hovered far too close to his ear. He could feel the warmth of the American woman's body far too close to his. And worse, he could feel betraying heat blooming over his cheeks.

"About what?"

His response was too brusque. The woman recoiled, her eyes wide and her mouth parting slightly.

She had a lovely mouth now that he looked more closely; plump lips with a gentle curve, and was that a dimple? He didn't dare drop his gaze any lower, not with that fire-engine red dress clinging to a body that was round in all the right places.

She chuckled. A deep-throated sound jerked his head up to meet her amused eyes, and he felt as if he was hooked on the end of a fishing line and she was reeling him in.

What a prize mullet he was, gaping at her like he had a schoolboy crush.

"Do you think it was interesting? I just uploaded the live recording. I'm sure I captured a few frames of you, too. I won't know until I check later," she added, tilting her head and smiling.

"Live? Me?" spluttered Jordan. Annoyance overrode his normal, easy-going, reticent nature. "I think anyone who videos themselves eating has got rocks in their head."

"Hey! That's my sister you're talking to!" Kirk scowled, half rising from his chair.

"Steady on, hero." Grinning, Billie placed a hand over where his rested, white-knuckled, on the table.

Pixie drawled, "Don't fuss, bro. I can handle this... this farm boy with one hand tied behind my back." She extended a bunched fist, saying, "Bump, bro."

A reluctant smile tugged her brother's mouth and he

nudged her knuckles with his own while Jordan rolled his eyes.

"Astraeus comes to mind, and Matilda agrees with me," intoned Ms Lette, fluttering her hands in the air and half-closing her eyes. "He's credited with being the creator of stars."

Oh no. Jordan cringed at the mention of Matilda, the ghost of Fig Tree Lodge and who, according to local gossip, was in constant contact with her direct descendent, Ms Lette, who rather fancied herself as a gifted fortune teller.

"Not again," said Mrs Brown while Tessa attempted to hide her giggle by holding a napkin up to her face.

Pixie glanced around the table and then asked, "Come again? I'm not sure I know what you're talking about?"

"You will. Let's have a toast, shall we? To the happy couple." Pushing to her feet, Ms Lette raised her glass, her words effectively splintering the curious silence that had fallen over everyone after her earlier statement had landed like a bomb in the room.

Everyone followed her lead, calling out a resounding chorus of *"To Billie and Kirk,"* and raising their glasses, while the old witch winked at Jordan before seating herself again.

Had she meant an entirely different couple from Billie and her fiancée? But who? No. He was imagining things. Giving a discrete shake of his head, Jordan placed his wine glass on the table as conversations resumed.

However, all noise ceased when Mrs Brown slapped a notebook down and clicked a ballpoint pen; the slight sounds acted like a bugle call to duty. Or maybe a rifle shot would be more apt.

Jordan swore he saw several people straighten in their chairs as if readying themselves to spring into action, the usual phenomenon whenever Mrs Brown and her best mate, Ms Lette, were the driving force on any committee.

"Let's discuss the Christmas in July event, shall we? Unless you and Kirk need any assistance planning your wedding, Billie?" Mrs Brown turned a fierce expression onto Billie, who quickly shook her head.

"No thanks, Mrs Brown. We're all good."

Kirk breathed an audible sigh, an expression of relief swamping his face when the older woman sniffed and flipped open her pad.

"Very well then," said Mrs Brown, sounding disappointed and clicking her pen like mad. "With only three weeks until the first of May, there's still much to sort out. We have cooking classes running throughout May, which Thea is organising, and I must say she is doing an excellent job sourcing volunteers. Beatrix and I have put our hands up for demonstrations on homemade jams, preserves and pickles and have booked the CWA hall for Friday mornings starting at 10.30 am. Sharp. Edwina, you can source a job lot of clean jars for participants to take their efforts home."

"If Grannie's helping, then so will I," announced Tilly, Tessa and Dodge's youngest daughter, flicking a carrot onto the floor. There was a snap of teeth as the small dog lurking near their feet gobbled it down. Her older sister, Kaylee, who sat next to her, giggled.

Pamela Brown said firmly, "Fridays are school days."

Tilly's little face turned red, but before she uttered another word, Ms Lette cut in.

"You and I are on picking duty."

"What's that, Grannie?" Now all smiles, the little girl turned adoring eyes on her grandmother.

"Every Thursday after school, we'll pick the vegetables and herbs from our garden for use in the class."

"I guess that's okay." Tilly kicked the chair with her feet, scowling as if she suspected she had been tricked.

"I don't think I can help this time, Mum." Kaylee frowned. "Last year in high school and all that."

"You could if you didn't spend each waking moment with your mates," Tessa said drily.

"We're studying!"

"Kaylee's got a boyfriend," sang Tilly.

"I have not!" Kaylee pulled Tilly's hair, making her squeal.

Dodge said, "Okay, girls. That's enough. Kaylee, aren't you too old for pulling hair?"

"Not when it comes to my little sister." She grinned as she spoke, tugged Tilly close and tickled her sides. Tilly's giggles made everyone smile.

The American woman leaned forward. "Cooking classes sound fun, especially if they use homegrown products. I'll do a podcast of myself learning to make my pickles. Where can I sign up? And what about you?"

She prodded Jordan in his ribs.

"Interested?"

Across the table, Kirk spluttered with barely suppressed amusement.

Jordan ground out, "I've got a job to do."

"Pity."

"Not all the classes are in the daytime. Maki's, for instance, will be held at night. Right here, in our kitchen at Fig Tree Lodge. You could come to the classes, Jordan, and afterwards, we can meet to discuss the wedding arrangements. Being part of the bridal party means a lot of behind-the-scenes work," Ms Lette said, her voice smug.

Before Jordan could stomp that suggestion into oblivion, Billie said, "I like that idea, Auntie Edwina, if it suits Mum. The timing is perfect; I won't have to even think about the wedding during the work week. We can sort it out Friday nights and have the weekend to do any needed running around."

Florrie Miller nodded. "Meeting on Friday nights to sort the wedding works for me, too."

"Excellent. Jordan and Pixie, I'll slot you both in for Maki's Japanese cooking classes." Mrs Brown scribbled away in her book while Jordan felt like a trapped worm in a bucket.

His mind raced, but for the life of him, he couldn't think of any reasonable objections.

Pixie's hand shot into the air, making vigorous waving motions, just missing whacking Jordan on the top of his head by a mere centimetre. "Oh, I do love Sushi. Yes, please, count me in."

Tessa leaned forward from where she sat further along the table. "You'll both still need to sign up officially. I'll send you the link to the online form I've made for the event."

Edwina Lette clapped her hands. "We're making excellent progress. Dodge, what's for dessert?"

Her grandson rose from the table, sporting a huge grin like he found the entire dinner extremely amusing. "Apple crumble with yoghurt. Everyone, remain where you are."

"Need any help?" Jordan fixed him with pleading eyes, but Dodge shook his head.

"I've got it covered, thanks mate."

Across from him, Billie wrinkled her nose and exchanged a look with her mother, who sat on her right-hand side. "What do you think about learning to cook some Sushi, Mum?"

Pastor Florrie Miller's nose quivered as she smiled. "I'll give it a go. What are the other cooking classes? Do you know Pam?"

"Hmm." Mrs Brown turned back a few pages. "There's Greek. Italian. Nepalese. And I believe Scottish."

"So many to choose from!" squealed Pixie. "I want to sign up for all of them!"

"We've got dress fittings, rehearsals, and the food to organise, but before we do all that, I want you to meet the rest of the bridal party," Kirk said.

"What? How many more? Since I'm the best woman, I thought I was it." Pixie poked her lower lip forward.

Jordan twitched in his chair when she caught him looking. He feigned disinterest by pretending to yawn behind his hand, then said, "I'm the chief bridesman."

"I'd forgotten that," she said slowly, as if some special meaning was behind the knowledge.

Billie said, "We've got two ordinary bridesmaids and two groomsmen."

"Do I know them?" Pixie looked at Billie.

"There's Tessa, of course."

"All present and account for!" Tessa waved, dark eyebrows quirking upwards.

"I'm not sure if you met Natalie Davidson when you were here last, Pixie. She's agreed to be my other bridesmaid. She's only been in town about five or six years, has a son, Noah and is now married to Troy, who is Auntie Edwina's ..." Here Billie paused, sending an enquiring glance towards the woman who was one of her mother's best friends and who she'd called 'auntie' since she was in nappies.

Edwina Lette nodded. "My cousin Janice's boy, which makes him Kirk and Pixie's second cousin, I think. Not that they had ever met until two years ago."

Billie pushed on. "Then there's Kaylee and Tilly, our flower girls. Then we have Kirk and Pixie's brother

Orlando, and lastly, a mate of Kirk's. You know everyone Jordan, apart from the two blokes from the US."

Jordan had always imagined Billie would choose a more bohemian approach whenever or if she decided to tie the knot. The manner in which this one was shaping surprised him.

"A very traditional wedding."

He instantly wished he could recant his words when Billie's eyes grew glassy as she looked at her parents, particularly her father, who was busy poking a fork beneath a slice of meat on his plate and lifting it as if searching for something.

"I always thought Dad would marry me, but now it's even better. Mum will do the honours as pastor, and Dad can walk me down the aisle."

"It'll be perfect, Billie," said Jordan softly, inwardly wincing when Kirk and his annoying sister shot him suspicious glances.

Dodge re-entered the room, bringing the scent of cinnamon and warm apples and pushing a tea trolley laden with bowls and a jug of yoghurt. The apple crumble rested on a crystal cake tray, and Jordan's mouth watered. Dodge had a reputation as a good cook. He served his two girls first, telling them they could leave the room after they'd finished their dessert.

Mrs Brown rapped the table with her knuckles. "I don't have all night. Next?"

"I've been thinking that a float parade through the town

might make a great drawcard for tourists when we begin advertising the whole Christmas in July thing. Anyone could join in; the scouts or local hobby groups, for instance, and we could have a band playing as they march down the streets."

"Good job, Tess." Dodge beamed at his wife with pride. "I'm sure the SES would be keen to participate, probably the firies as well."

"Yes! And provided there is some nod to Christmas, the floats could be decorated however they wish. Our local businesses can use it as a way of advertising their products or services. I'd love to set up a family float. I thought ours could have a historical slant; maybe an early Australian Christmas day or dinner? But I'm open to any other suggestions." Tessa glanced at her grandmother-in-law, who smiled approvingly.

Dodge butted in. "Plenty of old furniture and wares we can use from our shop for our float."

"Now you're talking! I love it!" Ms Lette added, "Pam. Send a text to the other CWA mob and tell them this is a goer."

Mrs Brown sniffed and clicked the top of her ball-point pen as if to make a point. "The committee has to vote, Edwina."

"Rubbish. Don't fuss, Pam. Everyone will get on board. It's something different. Tell 'em we can have a competition for the best-dressed float."

"And what will they win?"

No one spoke for a while, no doubt pondering ideas,

as Dodge ladled apple crumble and yoghurt into bowls before handing them around.

"A trophy? Or..." Jordan scratched his chin, a habit he had formed when he was young and which he had never been able to rid himself of.

"How about a weekend on a working farm, being shown how to milk a cow, feed the animals, make butter and cream? Would that be sufficiently fun enough to garner sufficient entries?" he said, thinking that he'd better run the idea past his parents before he offered their farm as the prize.

Tessa shook her head. "Not for the float parade. I assume locals will make up the bulk of the floats. But I think a farm weekend would be a great prize for any out-of-towners or tourists who enter other events; perhaps the karaoke night's final winner?"

"Sounds to me that the people who enter everything else you've got planned will most likely be locals, as you've already said, Tessa. But I like your idea, Jordan." Pixie shifted closer to Jordan, her right leg brushing against his thigh. She sent him an approving smile that had his heart skipping a beat and heat prickling his skin.

She rushed on, her voice high and excited.

"What if the mini farm holiday is used as a lucky door prize? All the tourists or out-of-towners can put their names down in some form, with the winner announced maybe on the last day of July. They would have to be able to choose what days would suit them when they want to claim the prize, however."

"Love it!" declared Ms Lette, cramming a spoonful of dessert into her mouth as she spoke. Her cheeks bulged, her eyes glittered as they rested on Pixie. And then, like a hungry crocodile hunting for its next meal, her gaze shifted to Jordan.

"Since we have more than enough on our plates, you two can be in charge of organising and promoting the farm weekend prize."

Stern Mrs Brown took down more notes.

A chuckling Dodge served Beatrix and Maki Fukuka their dessert.

Billie shot Jordan a sympathetic glance but then turned to her fiancée and gave him a besotted look, probably dismissing Jordan entirely from her mind.

While Pixie, the woman he had just met and the woman who, for the first time in far too many years, made him think of something other than his sheep, snatched up her phone, slung an arm around his shoulders, crying, "Smile, babe. More famous last words – I'm going to make you a star!"

Chapter Three

Despite the pale, watery sunbeams that flittered through the glass of the French doors, the bedroom remained chilly. Pixie, shivering under the covers, couldn't help but replay all that had occurred since her brother had picked her up at the bus terminal yesterday. The upcoming wedding had been a stroke of luck, prompting her to immediately board a plane to Sydney.

Imagine if she'd declined and decided to stay in the States - she could have missed what she firmly believed to be the opportunity of her lifetime. One she was determined to make the most of.

Accepting her brother's offer to be his best woman had been a turning point for Pixie. She was positive filming everything that would lead up to the wedding, all the work done behind the scenes, as well as the event itself, would be the catalyst she desperately needed to elevate her business to the next level, a testament to her business acumen.

That – and a small-town Christmas in July festival.

She mentally ticked off what had been planned so far and pondered how she could make the most of every experience: there was the wedding, of course, but she needed an angle to set the occasion apart from every other wedding. Sighing, she stared at the ceiling. The fact that the sexes were reversed for the best man and chief bridesmaid would work in her favour, but she needed more.

Maybe she could play up the lady pastor angle? But that was not so unusual these days. Maybe she could do a *'how to organise your wedding without breaking the bank'* type of spin? From conversations with her brother, she already knew they were working to a strict budget.

Putting a proverbial pin on the wedding event, she moved on to the town's plans.

There were cooking classes of various cuisines, karaoke nights, a Christmas play, and a Christmas-themed float parade. And there could be more the committee had scheduled that she didn't know about yet. She made another mental note to ask Edwina when the next meeting was due to be held. It would make an intriguing addition to her social media video clips about living in an Aussie country town if she could post a film revealing how the committee operated and how much of a part they played in small-town life.

Stretching her arms above her head, she emitted a happy whoop. She was going to be busy. The first thing she needed to do was compile a spreadsheet and brainstorm ways to ensure her video posts hit every note possible that would engage more followers and propel her career to the stratosphere. She made a mental note to include examples of some of the stranger Aussie idioms and slang terms in a few vids. Thanks to her brother's regular texts on the subject, she was already across many weird and wonderful things, which made conversing with her relatives much easier. For example, how chickens were called chooks!

Her mobile phone, which she had placed on her charger the previous night, emitted a short bird song. The coldness of the room was forgotten as she flung off the doona and snatched up the phone, fingers fumbling as she sought the information she craved.

Yes!

The short vids she had uploaded highlighting the first day of this visit were ticking upwards in a steady and very pleasing fashion.

But even better – the reel she had posted at the dinner table of her snuggling close to a granite-faced Jordan was the real winner. Over five thousand likes and still going strong, with a tonne of shares and a deluge of comments – the majority of which ran along the lines of *'who is that hot guy?'* and *'seriously crushing on him right now'*.

Who indeed?

Pixie stifled a giggle as she recalled the guy's totally flummoxed expression when she told him she would make him a star. Usually, she could get to the real meat of a person in under sixty seconds, a trait she prided herself on. But this Jordan guy was an enigma. The strong, silent type? Or was he simply a rude moron with no personality or social skills? Whoever he was, the tug deep in her belly and the flutter of her pulse every time she looked in his direction had been surprising, to say the least.

But one that she had no intention of making good on, she reminded herself. She was confident in her choices and current life path, and she had no doubt she was on the right track.

These days, career first was her motto.

Besides, she had always believed herself to be a one-man woman. And that man had already been and gone in her life, breaking her heart when he dumped her for her so-called best friend, Lisa.

She would show Chad what a terrible mistake he had made. She would show them exactly who they had turned their noses up at. She would be rich and famous and live such a fabulous lifestyle that they would spend the rest of their lives gnashing their teeth!

Which brought her back to reality with a thud. Time to get her skates on, which meant a quick vid to start the day. Maybe one of her brushing her teeth in the beautiful, vintage bathroom with its claw foot bath, marble tiles, gilt edged mirror and a chandelier of all things; as well as a super-comfy armchair with brocade upholstery and its own French doors leading to the veranda.

She tugged down the coral-coloured, oversized tee with a picture of a teddy bear on the front, which she always wore when sleeping and armed with her phone charged to the bathroom. Twenty minutes later, she was finally satisfied with the recording and, back in her room, uploaded it to her sites, noting with glee how she was instantly bombarded with likes, love hearts and shares.

Perfect!

Smiling, she chose a pair of pale blue jeans and a sage green pullover, then tugged on thick socks and her white tennis shoes. Some attention to her face and hair and she was done. As she surveyed herself in the mirror before leaving her room, the image of Jordan popped into her head again, and how he had seemed to flush each time he looked at her.

Her followers were right.

He *was* cute.

She rather liked his firm square chin and the curve of his lips when he smiled, which, let's face it, was not often. And those brown eyes of his were like liquid pools of melted dark chocolate.

She squirmed a little. Okay, she'd accept he was hot with those broad muscular shoulders and stocky build that made her think he was the kind of man who could carry the weight of the world and not buckle under the pressure.

Then she snorted. She squared her shoulders and flung back her head, slamming the bedroom door as she exited; and in doing so, vanquished those silly thoughts.

He was just a man.

He was no one special.

A couple of hours later, she was seated at a table outside the Cyprus Café and enjoying an amazingly good coffee with Tessa, Natalie and a blonde woman in her forties who had been introduced as Abby Taylor and who was dressed in a police uniform.

Tessa, who appeared to be a born organiser, brought out a tablet and began tapping away at the screen.

"Thanks heaps, ladies, for coming at such short notice."

"No worries," said Abby, cupping both hands around her mug and half-closing her eyes as she inhaled the rich aroma. "Anything to get out of more paperwork. Area command has requested a heap of reports and, as usual, given us little time to compile."

"Will our committee's plans for July mean you'll have even more to do?" Tessa looked to her friend, sympathy warming her brown eyes.

Abby shrugged. "Comes with the territory. It'll be apples. How's Noah doing at uni, Nat?"

"Loving the subjects he chose but not liking being away from home, even though Tamworth is close enough he can return on the weekends. Not much we can do about that though; we're very grateful that he was able to board with a family your parents know, Billie," said Natalie.

"Mum was happy to help. She thinks a lot of Noah."

"Still, Troy and I are relieved knowing our son will be looked after. Even better, Drew is boarding with them, too. Made everything so much easier when both boys obtained places at the same university."

"What's Noah studying again?" asked Tessa.

Natalie huffed out a breath and grimaced. "A bachelor of Sustainability, and he hopes to major in Environmental Science. I know, right? This came totally out of the blue. For a while there, he was so gung-ho about going into the Army. It was all he talked about."

"I know exactly what you mean. Kaylee's been interested in studying astronomy for so long, I thought it was a done deal." Tessa chuckled and spread her hands. "But only yesterday, she mentioned looking into acting school in Sydney."

"Still, it's tough when they're not with you. Drew keeps raving about how awesome his media course is, and I'm so proud of him for pursuing his dreams. But that doesn't stop me from missing him every day. At least Kaylee has until the end of the year before she applies anywhere," Abby said.

"Yeah, it will be a huge adjustment for us when she

leaves home. We're just making the most of every moment we're with her. Although these days, that's not so much; she's either out horse riding or with her bestie, Gillian." Tessa blinked rapidly and then cleared her throat.

"Moving on - I invited you today, Abby because I wanted a police perspective about our float / parade idea; you know, keeping order, barricading off streets for several hours – that kind of thing."

"Shouldn't be a problem. Remember the Queen's birthday parade we had several years ago? Went like clockwork."

"If it takes off, this parade could be bigger," warned Tessa.

Abby smiled. "I think it's a great idea. As soon as you've settled on a date and time, let me know, and I'll send you through any permits that need to be completed. Then, we'll work up a plan. When I told Roman, he fired off so many ideas for the SES I couldn't keep up; he even wants us coppers to have a float."

"That would be perfect and a good way of fermenting goodwill for the police force. Our local Sheriff's department participates annually in our town's Fourth of July parade." Pixie tapped the table with a long, polished red nail. "I know I'm new here and only a guest for a short while, but I'd love to help wherever possible."

Tessa glanced at Natalie, who promptly said, "Happy to hear your input on the family float, Pixie. After all, you're more a Lette than me, given I've only married into the family."

Tessa grinned. "Like me."

Abby finished the last of her coffee with a sigh, setting the mug onto the table. "If we get our head honcho's approval, I'm sure a police float will be a goer. That said, we'd love your help if you can squeeze us in, too. AJ is the only one with no immediate family to take up his spare time, and I'm not particularly imaginative. I wouldn't know where to start."

"I've got some ideas."

Abby grinned at Pixie.

"Somehow I knew you'd say that."

"We've got our bridal party commitments, too, Pixie." Tessa frowned as she swept a thumb over her tablet, then lowered her voice and added, "I'm glad Billie cried off coming here this morning because I'd like to discuss a rather delicate matter without her presence."

Pixie's brows rose as her mind raced with all sorts of possibilities. "Delicate? Like how so?"

"As well as all the formal stuff, I want to give Billie a surprise bridal shower slash baby shower party."

Pixie's mouth sagged as she goggled at the other woman. Her brother was going to be a daddy. She was going to be an aunt! Now, that – was not what she had expected.

"Oh my ...! I don't believe it! When did this happen? How...I mean..." Heat scalded her face when the other women chuckled, and then she sniggered when her words finally registered.

"Scrap that - I really don't want to know the answer. I meant to say I had no idea. Kirk has told me nothing. I wonder if Mom and Dad know?"

Tessa laid a cold hand over Pixie's, no trace of any amusement on her face now. "No one else knows apart from me. And that was only because I caught Billie puking in the loos at our CWA meeting last Monday. Naturally, Kirk is aware, but I'm not sure about her mum. All I know is that Billie doesn't want to announce her news until she's past the three-month trimester – meaning sometime in early May. She's a bit concerned about being a first-time mum at forty-one years old. Now, ladies, this is the deal. I've been sworn to secrecy and am now swearing you three to secrecy, too."

"I'm a cop. I do secrets particularly well." Abby grinned, also keeping her voice soft.

Beaming, Natalie crossed her heart with her gloved fingers and murmured, "I'm so happy for her. For them both. I won't say a word."

Then Tessa turned to Pixie, indicating with a jerk of her chin to where Pixie's mobile phone lay on the table.

"Kirk has mentioned that you're an influencer, and I understand that's how you make your living. However, I know you've been uploading videos of our home, but I don't know if Gran is aware of what you're doing. Fig Tree Lodge is our home, and I had hoped you would treat it and us respectfully."

The warmth that had flushed Pixie's cheeks only a few moments ago chilled as she took in the serious expressions surrounding her. Natalie fiddled with her mug while the policewoman stared across the table at her with cool eyes.

Pixie lifted her head. "I'll talk to Edwina today. I'm sure it won't be a problem. It's only pictures of the house and the grounds."

"Okay, but I don't want any images of my daughters floating about online."

The firm note of warning in the other woman's voice rang through clearly, and Pixie's fingers closed over her phone in a tight clench. "What about the wedding, though? Aren't they the flower girls?"

"True." Tessa paused, obviously thinking through possible scenarios. "No, I'm sorry, Pixie. If they appear in any of your shots or recordings, I'd like them to be edited out."

"Got it."

Tessa's face turned fierce as she pinned Pixie with a look that was strongly reminiscent of grandmother-in-law, Edwina Lette. "You see, I almost lost my eldest daughter because of someone posting footage of me online that enabled a psychopath to hunt us down. So, this is very important to me."

"No, I totally understand." Pixie nodded vigorously and smiled.

But Tessa's serious expression didn't change as she

continued, the timbre of her tone so quiet Pixie had to lean closer to hear.

"Now, about Billie and Kirk's baby news - you seriously cannot mention anything to anyone, especially on your social media sites. Not even a hint. If not posting about this news will be a problem for you, I'll have Abby confiscate your phone and your laptop."

"What? She can do that?"

More than a little stung that Tessa could think that she'd be such a poor future sister-in-law to Billie, Pixie bristled, all her senses on high alert as she sprang into defence mode.

Abby hooked her thumbs in her thick police-issued vest and declared in a sotto voice, "I do what it takes to look after my mates."

Head high, Pixie gathered her things and stood, aware that a table full of elderly women were craning their necks as if trying to listen as they stole furtive glances in their direction. She remembered how her bestie had betrayed her and made her look like a fool in front of everyone she knew. How heartbroken she'd been, her dreams shattered, the life she thought she'd live - in ruins.

"You ambushed me."

Tessa also pushed to her feet and held her hands out, almost like an offering. But an offering of what?

"Yes, I did rather. But the thing is, I don't know you very well, so I had to be honest and let you know where I stand. I certainly didn't mean anything personal or indicate in any way that you couldn't be trusted. I apologise if I indicated anything contrary. Family is everything to me, and you are part of my family. It's my dearest wish that we will become firm friends. What about you? Do you think we could be friends?"

Her words rang with sincerity, her gaze steady, even a little anxious.

Her nails dug into her palms, and Pixie clutched her mobile phone to her chest as she searched Tessa's face before checking out the other women.

No hint of any smirks.

No hint of any evasion in their open gazes.

In fact, they all looked rather worried.

More than that, they looked concerned – concerned for Pixie.

Maybe Tessa was right to be cautious about her motives, especially given the woman's history with social media and how some crazy had threatened her daughter.

Then there was the fact that Pixie still hadn't checked with Edwina even though she *had* promised Kirk and Billie yesterday that she would do so. In hindsight, she admitted she hadn't exactly covered herself in glory by being open about her activities.

Tessa had laid her cards on the table.

It had been a long time since anyone, apart from Pixie's own family, had been so honest with her.

It had been a long time since anyone had been a true friend.

As Pixie stood hugging her phone and shivering in

the bitter wind, looking from face to face, some of the stiffness flowed from her cold body.

"I'd like that – I'd like to be friends."

But even as she maintained a pleasant expression as she looked to the other women who grinned back, relief soothing the tightness from their features, Pixie couldn't help wondering whether *she* could trust them.

Chapter Four

On Saturday, the day after the local Anzac Day march, Jordan attended the Bindarra Creek SES building for a general meeting their captain, Roman Taylor, had scheduled. It meant that he had to rise before dawn and not stop until all the farm chores for that day had been completed, especially as the day before had been a short workday given that his parents and he had attended the march. He didn't mind, though, as he had a fair idea about the agenda. Their captain always called for a meeting around this time of year, and it was always about the same thing – volunteers to source firewood for the coming winter, which would be distributed free of charge to those who needed it. It was also an excellent method of ridding his property of fallen trees and deadwood. Win, win, in Jordan's opinion.

Enjoying the current song on the local radio, he pulled into the SES parking lot and gazed with satisfaction at the decent number of cars and utes already parked up. He climbed out of his dual-cab ute, grabbed his jacket off the passenger seat, and strode into the building, greeting people as he passed through the crowd.

The atmosphere was casual and upbeat.

There was no natural disaster to prepare for, which was a nice change after a long summer spent assisting the rural fire brigade in back-burning and making fire breaks around the region.

Before he took a seat, he made himself a cup of tea using the urn that was always on the boil and a generic no-name tea bag.

Turning, he found himself standing next to Kirk, and for a couple of beats, an awkward silence lay between them until Jordan cleared his throat.

"Billie here, too?"

The other bloke's eyes narrowed. "No, she's doing a special training day with her apprentice."

"Oh, right. Bing's boy, Ethan."

"I guess it takes being born here to know everyone or be considered a local."

"Not really. We're pretty accepting of newcomers. Wasn't that long ago, the town was all but dead. People moving to the city looking for better jobs or better pay, even better health facilities. Several years ago, we had a big push to entice more people into the area; luckily, the campaign was successful, and Bindarra keeps growing. A good half of the town hasn't been here that long." Jordan blew over his hot, inky black and strong tea exactly how he liked it.

Although they had met several times, including when he attended the engagement party, he barely knew the guy next to him. Any in-depth conversation at the engagement had never eventuated; the large private room at the RSL had been packed, and at the time, Jordan had been dealing with the knowledge that any hope he may have harboured of a happy ever after with Billie was as dead as a doornail. Of course, he had heard all the gossip about her fiancée's former career, but there was always gossip in Bindarra Creek. Didn't mean any of it was true. Still, the bloke's history had piqued his own curiosity.

"What about yourself? Think you and Billie will make this your home? Or are you thinking of returning later to the States?"

"No. Billie's heart belongs here, so I'm here to stay. You're not going to get rid of me any time soon."

"Hey! I didn't mean anything by that – I was curious, that's all."

Kirk nodded slowly. "All right then."

"We were good mates in school, you know. Billie and I. I'm glad she's met someone who makes her happy."

As soon as he said the words, Jordan realised he meant them. Which was odd considering that he had spent most of his life pining a little for her. Then he grinned as he recalled a particular tidbit of gossip. "Were you really an actor in a daytime soapy?"

"You got me." Kirk chuckled. "Paid the bills, and I thought it would be a solid stepping stone into the big time. But when Hollywood finally called, I realised that wasn't the life I wanted or needed. So here I am."

"Here we both are – about to be roped into more work. Hope you're not afraid of drop bears," Jordan said with a straight face.

Kirk laughed. "Can't catch me out on that one. Dodge beat you to the punch."

"I'll get you next time." Jordan grinned. "Looks like we're about to start. Catch you later."

He dipped his chin and edged towards a vacant chair as the SES captain, Roman Taylor, raised his hand for silence.

The meeting went exactly as Jordan had envisaged. Names were taken, and locations were pinned down for the firewood scavenge. This was then followed by a rowdy discussion of the SES having a float in the Christmas in July parade to be held on Thursday, 19th July. More names were taken down for designing and decorating the float.

It wasn't until the meeting was convened and the area thinned out of people that Jordan noticed Pixie. She was chatting animatedly with her brother and Roman while – naturally – filming the inside of the SES building. The way he had looked for her in the crowds lining the main street yesterday for the march had been, in his mind, pathetic. He'd been so sure that he'd run into her that she couldn't resist filming the march, but somehow, their paths hadn't crossed, and he'd returned home after lunching at the RSL club with his parents more than a little flat and irritated with himself.

And now she was here, the last place he thought he'd find her.

For a split second, Jordan entertained the craven thought of escaping before he was spotted, then he squared his shoulders and marched over, telling himself he had a few things to discuss with the SES Captain. But the truth was, her presence was a fascination he couldn't resist.

Roman nodded as he approached, then continued giving an overview of the SES's vital role in the community, tacking on a brief rundown of the cleanup required after a recent motor vehicle accident the team had attended. All interspersed with short exclamations and studied serious expressions on Pixie's face as she filmed the interview.

Winding down, Roman thrust out his hand, shook hers and muttered something about seeing a bloke about a car.

Without missing a beat, Pixie spun her mobile around to face Jordan, her eyes twinkling over the top of the plastic device.

"Babe! Just the man I need to see. Now let's have your personal insight into the selfless work the SES does; what is your most outstanding moment?"

She was filming him! Did the woman ever not have that phone in her hands?

"Do you mind?" he growled.

She peeped around the phone, a smirk tugging at her lips.

"No. Do you?"

"Actually, yes. Please turn it off."

Rolling her eyes and making a moue of her mouth simultaneously, Pixie huffed out a breath but did acquiesce.

"Now, who's a grumpy bear?"

Wondering why on earth he had thought it might be a good idea to enter her vicinity, he shoved his hands into his pockets, hunching his shoulders against the afternoon's chill, unable to think of a way to extricate himself. And worse, knowing he was reluctant to leave anyway despite his misgivings.

"Do you mind, Jordan, if I have a word with my sister?" Kirk looked from one to the other.

"No worries, I'll make myself scarce."

"I'm sure that as part of the bridal party, Jordan should also hear what you say." And before he could move, Pixie linked an arm through his, snuggling close in a proprietorial manner.

Yep, the woman did not have a clue about personal space.

She said, "See? Two against one. Whatever you're going to say, I warn you, bro, you're outnumbered."

Picking up on the constrained tone in Kirk's voice,

Jordan wondered what bomb was about to fall on his head this time. "Is there a problem?"

"No, of course not." Kirk spread his hands wide. "Let's find somewhere a bit quieter."

Pixie drawled, "Sounds ominous! Here will do."

A quick glance sideways revealed the tiny frown creasing her forehead and the tension radiating from her stiff body.

"I want to ask Chad if he'll be one of my groomsmen." The words came out in a rush, accompanied by Kirk jabbing a foot into the dirt like a nervous kid in the schoolyard.

Jordan's inner radar pricked up its ears.

"And...?" The muscles where Pixie's arm pressed against his were rock hard.

"I thought I'd check before I contacted him if this would ... bother you."

Pixie trilled a laugh. "Why would it?"

Kirk sighed. "You know why."

"It's fine, bro. Go for it. See you later. I'll catch a lift back to the Lodge with Jordan." Whirling around, she tugged Jordan into motion and all but dragged him towards the car park.

Jordan looked over his shoulder to see Kirk staring after them and running a hand through his hair.

"What was that all about?"

"Oh, you know. The usual. Old flame and all that." She tossed her head like it was yesterday's news and meant nothing.

But he wasn't fooled. He paused beside his ute and, turning to face her, caught a glimpse of overbright eyes. Damn, were those tears?

"Hey." His voice was gentle as he knuckle-nudged her gently beneath her chin. "You, okay?"

She sniffed, then nodded. "I wasn't expecting that one."

"Want to talk about it?"

"There's not much to say. Chad is Kirk's school buddy, and he was a big part of my brother's life when I was growing up. Which meant he was a big part of mine. I always had a bit of thing for him, so I thought all my dreams had come true when he asked me out at my eighteenth birthday party."

"Yeah. I know all about those kinds of relationships." His mind immediately winged to Billie, memories of their schooldays together bombarding him like sharp arrows.

Her expression was grave as she searched his face. "I figured as much."

He gave a wry smile. "Like to share more? No pressure if you don't want to. I totally get about keeping some aspects of your life private."

"Hmm. But you can be too private, you know, babe?" She tilted her head, considering him. "It's important to open yourself to others. That's what connecting is all about."

Jordan sucked in a deep, slow breath. "I don't think

you've been practising what you're preaching. Otherwise, why would your brother have to ask?"

"Good point. I'll give you that one."

The shadows in her eyes lessened, a little of their usual sparkle returning as she smiled - a smile that sizzled through to his bones and made him think thoughts that had nothing to do with a chilly afternoon standing around the SES carpark.

"Okay. Here goes." Her happy beam dimmed a little as she continued. "We dated for two years, and just when I thought he was going to pop the big question – he did – except not to me. To my best friend."

"Strewth...!" Jordan reached out and placed a gentle hand on her shoulder.

"That would have been a hell of a shock."

"You're telling me! I didn't see it coming. Maybe I should have, but..." Pixie shrugged. "It turned out that I trusted both of them too much."

"At that age, you would have had to re-think your entire life," Jordan said slowly.

She nodded. "Exactly. Their betrayal turned everything I thought I knew about myself on its head. Suddenly, I wasn't so sure of myself, who I was and worse, what value I had."

Then she paused, frowning a little as she met his steady gaze.

"I don't know why I'm telling you all this – it's not as if we've known each other for very long. But somehow...I feel as if you would understand."

"I do understand." His voice was low as if they had been gauged from deep within his soul. Standing beside this woman, something shifted inside, tearing down walls he'd spent almost a lifetime building. His light clasp on her shoulder tightened for a moment. Then, just as he was about to allow his touch to fall away, she reached up and laid her hand over his. With a sense of wonder, Jordan forgot where he stood, surrounded by people he'd known forever but hadn't really known at all, mainly because of the barriers he'd built after experiencing his own rejection.

Throat dry, he croaked out, "I grew up thinking that Billie and I would be together forever. But it never happened."

"Oh, Jordan. That sucks." Her eyes glistened wetly.

She was so close not even a breeze could flutter between them.

He added, "I thought for a long time that I was never enough."

"You thought wrong."

Moistening her lips with the tip of her tongue, she all but whispered, "I know what that's like. You see, Lisa was so much more – more of everything than me. Prettier, thinner, but what had been the crunch where Chad was apparently concerned, she was the daughter of a very influential man with a sizeable trust fund. Then, the guy made billions in the crypto market when it was in its infancy. It was a fact that Lisa took great joy in broadcasting to me whenever we crossed paths. I have felt invisible for so long."

He leaned forward, resting his forehead on hers. "I see you."

"Ditto, babe."

She sighed the words, "How strange that we do have something in common after all."

"I know, right? It does feel a bit ... weird."

Clearing his throat, he suddenly realised where he was and what he was doing, standing with his forehead pressed to hers with all his mates gawking on. And, worse, he was baring his soul to a crazy social media fanatic. What if he ended up being tomorrow's news all over the internet?

With a jerky motion, he stepped away, dropping her hands, heat flooding his face as he snuck furtive glances around the carpark. He cringed at the sight of Dodge, Troy, AJ and Professor Callen snickering and giving each other the old elbow nudge.

But either Pixie hadn't seen their audience, or she didn't care.

Giggling, she ducked her head, bringing up her phone and placing it in front of her face in such a way that he couldn't help but think she used it as a trick to hide her true self from the world.

"Now, come on. Give me a smile and tell me one of your hero stories."

"I'm no hero."

She peeped out over the top of her mobile, eyes

glinting wickedly. "Depends on a person's version of being a hero, doesn't it?"

Unable to help himself, he chuckled. "What's yours?"

"Oh, I don't know. Maybe a guy who can listen and empathise. Trust me, babe, that's worth more than cold hard cash in my book."

"Glad to hear it."

Raising his brows, he tapped the top of her phone. "Then why are you so hung up on making money?"

The laughter in her face faded as she lowered the phone.

"I thought that would be obvious."

But he shook his head and pulled out his car keys. "If you're still trying to prove something to that douchebag who dumped you, then you're not over him. You're stuck in the past, and it doesn't matter how wealthy you are; you'll never be able to move forward."

"Wow. Listen to you! I'm not the only one who can't move forward. Do you think no one notices those cow eyes you turn on Billie all the time? It's embarrassing."

And poof, just like that, up went his walls again.

Shoulders stiff, lips thin, he yanked open the car door. "I'll give you that lift home."

"Don't bother. I can walk."

Head high, Pixie stalked out of the SES carpark leaving Jordan wondering where all those warm and fuzzy feelings had disappeared to. And what the devil had he done wrong.

<h1 style="text-align:center">Chapter Five</h1>

Later that same Saturday night, Billie and Kirk arrived at the Lodge after dinner to pin down dates and times for dress fittings, rehearsals, and meetings about the reception which was going to be held in the grounds of Fig Tree Lodge. Dodge, his father Warren and stepmother Lou were in charge of the catering, although the happy-couple-to-be had yet to decide on the menu. During that meeting, Pixie was issued with Jordan's mobile phone number. Apparently, once Edwina had paired her with him as a *'team'*, everyone else assumed she would pass on any updates on the wedding or the Christmas in July festival.

Their heated exchange in the SES car park had lingered in Pixie's mind, disrupting her sleep and prompting a revaluation of her life choices. She oscillated between anger at Jordan's audacity to judge her and hurt at his apparent low opinion of her. But these emotions were overshadowed by the memory of their discussion about their past loves.

Chad and Billie.

A tide of shame flowed over her whenever she recalled the words she had flung in Jordan's face – which was often. Sure, the guy did go a bit soft whenever he looked at Billie, but every time Pixie imagined the expression on his face, she couldn't help but compare it to the heated glances he sent her.

Yeah, he may well have harboured some school kid crush on his best buddy, but Pixie suspected that was all it had ever been.

And then he sure had been sweet when he'd offered her emotional support in the SES carpark.

He had stood so close that she could feel his energy and body warmth. She had wasted a good portion of the night and a lot of nights since, wondering what his kiss would be like, how his lips would feel on hers, how he would taste.

Consequently, Pixie was angsting over her first text to Jordan on Sunday morning. She'd woken feeling grumpy and miserably surveyed the bags under her bloodshot eyes in the bathroom mirror. In the end, that first message to him had been abrupt and to the point.

But to her amazement, he had swiftly responded with a thumbs-up, followed by a formal and super brief apology for his words the previous day, saying he had no intention of causing any hurt or embarrassment.

The result was she was one confused gal over the next couple of weeks to such an extent she hardly spared a thought to the fact that soon she'd be face to face with the man who had broken her heart all those years ago. No – it was that farmer who was an itch she couldn't scratch enough to get rid of. Not that she allowed herself to sit and wallow. That wasn't in her nature. Despite her inner turmoil, she remained resilient and focused on her goal. She had a business to run, a tonne of cooking classes to attend, as well as helping her family with the Christmas in July festival.

Her days were busy, overflowing with conversations with family, being introduced to more of the townsfolk, and diving headfirst into PA mode to help Tessa. The latter, of course, also meant more brief texts to Jordan about the family float for the parade. When they hit the roadblock of transporting the float, Jordan offered the use of his flat-bed truck, which Edwina quickly accepted. He'd indicated his vehicle was a good twenty metres long with an extra wide bed and would be the perfect platform for their set.

Where once she would have yawned herself silly over the idea of anyone enjoying living in a small town, now she began to revise that opinion. Each encounter opened her eyes to how these folk lived and connected with each other, rather like the Mississippi River with its numerous estuaries, which she had explored one winter with a group of preppers. All those channels that fed off and linked with the one source united the locals in a way she'd never appreciated or thought about. She'd grown to love the town's slower pace and how, while most folks had a full schedule each day, they still found time to stop in the street and have a lengthy chat, meet up for a hot drink, attend various activities like the yoga class Tessa ran; or indulge in different hobbies such as painting classes in the park.

It struck her one bitterly cold afternoon when she was helping an old couple, who insisted she call them by their first names, Ted and Betty, back from the super-market with their shopping, that this was the first time in her life that she felt...fulfilled. They invited her into their small home, where they plied her with buttered scones and hot tea while reminiscing about events in the town and their courtship that had happened so long ago. To her surprise, not once during that lovely visit did she even consider recording any of it onto her phone, let alone telling the world via her sites about it. When she said her goodbyes, she noticed that someone had left a pile of fire-wood stacked neatly on the front porch. Betty divulged how grateful she was that the SES supplied the firewood free of charge every winter.

And that comment brought Jordan front and centre into her mind - again.

Not that he had rarely left it!

Still, Pixie had vowed long ago to spend as little time as possible moping after a guy, and it was with that noble intention in her mind that she trotted off to the first cooking class sessions, where she had a total hoot.

It was held in the Cyprus Café on a Monday night, where Vito revealed his secrets about making genuine Italian meals. What made the event even more pleasurable was that her relatives, Tessa and Edwina, accompanied her. They met up with Billie's mother there, and who Pixie quickly realised was much more than a pastor. Florrie Miller possessed an inquiring mind and was highly educated in philosophy and her chosen career of religion. It wasn't hard to see why the woman was popular in town, both with her congregation and her large circle of friends – for one, she never judged and was renowned as a bit of a peacemaker. She was also an excellent shot – which just about blew Pixie's mind when she heard about the many exploits and achievements of the Bindarra Creek Women's Target Rifle Shooting Club (seriously! What a mouthful!).

Of course, once the cooking lesson finished, most participants decided to hang around, gossip, and gorge themselves on what they had made this first lesson — egg pasta with a basic Bolognese sauce, finishing up with Struffoli — two ways. That dessert was so scrumptious, sweet, and zesty, her favourite flavours, that Pixie could have eaten everyone's serving, not just her own.

Adhering to Vito's request, she restricted her filming to a short clip of the café's exterior before they entered the building and one photo of the food.

The next night, she trotted along with Tessa and

Natalie to the Country Women's Association Hall, which she had quickly learnt to call by its acronym CWA, for a Scottish cooking class. The lure of learning how to make a Tipsy Laird dessert was something Pixie could not pass on and which didn't disappoint.

The following night, she found herself back at the Cyprus Café, this time with Abby Taylor, discovering the tantalising world of Greek food and some seriously awesome baklava. Then, Thursday night, she enjoyed her first taste of Nepalese cuisine in Ishya's kitchen with the formidable Mrs Brown and Natalie. There, she was introduced again to Dr Fatima Maloof, the local dentist, and her new husband, Professor Ernest Callen, who were firm friends of Natalie's. Everyone was warm and welcoming, and it felt much like being enfolded in a comfortable, soft blanket. Gradually, her barriers lowered as she became more personally involved with other people, which was a big step for someone who had spent much of her life on the perimeter looking in.

Pixie was in two minds about her opinion of Jordan – whether he was one of those still waters run deep kind of guy or a socially inept one. But while she knew she didn't want to waste too much time pondering that question (an internal lecture that failed miserably); she hoped for the former – a lot. It was with that tantalising dilemma still occupying her mind that she trotted into the CWA hall Friday morning, keen to experience her first lesson on preserving food and making jam. Hot on her heels came Edwina with Tilly, skipping beside her and carrying a basket overflowing with freshly picked fruit from the home garden. Both Edwina and Pixie held cardboard boxes containing sterilised glass jars for the participants to take their efforts home. A healthy number of people of varying ages were already in the hall. She called out a cheery hello when she spotted Ted and Betty who were well rugged up against the cold with overcoats that swamped their thin frames.

Tessa darted into the hall and pried a reluctant Tilly from her grandmother's side. She said good luck to everyone before tugging her daughter out the door and off to school. At breakfast that morning, she'd acquiesced to Tilly's constant begging to help Grannie and had organised for her daughter to start school later that day – as a one-off treat.

A silent spectator to the noisy scene, Pixie had been in awe. Before now, her experience with children was zilch. Living in Fig Tree Lodge these past weeks had been a real eye-opener for her at how demanding and complicated parenting could be; she was in complete admiration for Tessa and Dodge's great job with how they raised their two daughters. And also had to hold in a lot of laughter when Edwina either stirred the pot or soothed the troubled waters. But what affected her the most was how tight their family unit was and the level of loving tolerance and respect that existed between them.

Another whole new experience for her was viewing the dynamics of the Brown and Fukuka household and learning about their history. The tragic story of how Mrs

Pamela Brown had lost her husband and only child to floods years ago and had never re-married stirred her empathy and opened her eyes to the prickly older woman. Then, the story of how her spinster younger sister fell in love at sixty-five with Tessa's elderly mentor, Maki Fukuka and how they had married a few months later. They all lived together in the sisters' house and, with Tessa's skills, had built up a moderately successful online business selling homemade wine from products they grew themselves - which rather blew Pixie's mind. Their lives were a testament that it was never too late. Their history was so amazing that their stories inspired and humbled her.

She also discovered that she relished and admired Pamela Brown's no-nonsense attitude. The woman had a fantastic, dry humour and a well-camouflaged kind heart. She thought the old lady liked her as well, and she had been touched when Mrs Brown had agreed to have Pixie pick her up in her rental car each week so they could attend Ishya's cooking class together.

The first lesson that day was on the various ways to preserve food. Pixie scribbled notes until her hand ached; even though handouts had been given, there were often titbits added that hadn't been included, and she was determined not to miss a single thing. Her table partner was Dr Maloof, who asked her to call her Fatima, and they were soon sniggering as they worked together chopping cabbage, onions, and gherkins and stuffing them into sterilised jars. They added salt and water to the cabbage jars and vinegar, which they had to boil on the stove, and then dill to the gherkins. The onions they pickled with a mixture of vinegar, water, sugar and salt.

When the lesson finished, both Pixie and Fatima were pleased with their efforts.

"That was so much fun," said Fatima as she shoved her arms into her coat sleeves. "Are you coming next week?"

Pixie grinned, wiping moisture off the outside of a pickled onion jar. "Definitely. Yourself?"

Fatima nodded. "Wouldn't miss it. I could pick you up if you like?"

"I'd love that, thank you."

"Excellent. Oh, here's my card. It has my mobile number on it. We could do coffee sometime, perhaps?"

"Again – another yes, please."

"I must go. Ernest and I are taking the girls out to the caves to explore tomorrow, so I want all the housework done today. And their homework." Fatima gave a wry grin, adjusted her hot pink Hijab and hustled out of the hall.

Looking after her, Pixie marvelled that she had made another friend before moving to the elderly sisters and asking what she could do to help.

After the last participant had left, they spent the next thirty-odd minutes clearing up. Dodge arrived to stack and reposition the tables and chairs while Edwina, Florrie and Beatrix trotted to and fro, packing the leftover produce and containers. Pixie insisted on doing the washing up, which was considerable, generated from the complimentary tea and coffee and homemade snacks generously donated by Mrs Brown and Mrs Fukuka. She stood at the sink chatting with Mrs Brown, who narrowly inspected each plate she was handed before wiping them dry with a dish towel. One half of her was listening with awe as the older woman advised her on the best method of brewing your own wine while making a mental note to interview the lady, not for any social media post she hoped to make, but instead for her own benefit. The process sounded fascinating, and the prospect of making wine from something you had grown in your garden was tantalising. Pixie decided, then and there, to add it to her Life's Bucket list. While wiping down the sink and chasing the last suds down the drain as Mrs Brown put away the plates, she allowed her thoughts to turn to that night's event.

The first Japanese cooking class was held in the kitchen at Fig Tree Lodge.

But what really consumed her rioting imagination was the knowledge that tonight - she'd see Jordan again.

And she couldn't wait.

Chapter Six

The first Japanese cooking class held in Fig Tree Lodge's kitchen, with Maki Fukuka as the chef, went off with a bang. There were no other words for it. And despite his reservations about eating raw fish, Jordan had enjoyed the experience so much that he looked forward to the next session. He'd been late arriving as he'd been held up by a last-minute minor crisis involving a sheep, a dam, and a lot of mud, but that had been sorted with the sheep no worse for its experience. After a quick shower and change of clothes, he'd driven into Bindarra Creek to find he'd missed the first fifteen minutes of the lesson.

Not that he'd missed much, as whispered to him by Pixie, who had stationed herself at his side the moment he appeared.

And who'd remained there ever since.

Not that he wanted to complain about that – he'd seen nothing of her since that SES meeting two weeks ago when the firewood scavenging detail had been nutted out. That didn't mean that she hadn't snuck into his thoughts when he wasn't being vigilant! Of course, it hadn't helped when she'd somehow obtained his mobile number and sent him a couple of updates concerning the progress of Billie's wedding arrangements. His responses had been terse and to the point, no *'how are you's'*, no banal remarks about the weather, no *'let's catch up for coffee'*. But he had apologised by text for his dumb comment to her about being unable to move on from her ex, which, if he was honest, had been playing on his mind, making him feel ashamed he'd resorted to childish tit-for-tat measures. She had responded with a brief smiley face emoji – which told him nothing. Their following exchanges had been polite but impersonal.

Throwing himself into everything he could think of to keep himself so tired at the end of the day that he'd fall instantly asleep and wouldn't think about her hadn't been quite the success he had hoped.

Somehow, the image of her cheeky grin and dazzling green eyes would just not leave his head.

But they were obligated to meet up several times until the big day when his best friend wed her brother, so avoiding her was not an option. He'd assumed that would amount to about two or three occasions, but now he wasn't so sure. Especially since they had both become tied together as an organising team for the town's Christmas in July festival. As the days passed, he began questioning more and more whether he genuinely wanted to keep her at a distance.

Which brought him here to Fig Tree Lodge on a Friday night when he was usually at the pub watching the footy on a big screen, enjoying a cold beer, and being in the company of a couple of mates. Instead, he was learning how to make sticky rice and having a bloody good time with Pixie giggling by his side. She'd been curious as to why he'd been late and shown an interest that felt to Jordan as genuine when he'd given a brief rundown on his sheep problem. The gentle squeeze she'd given his forearm and her query over the sheep's prognosis had made him feel that she cared and had done nothing to eradicate his complicated feelings towards her. She'd proven to be a fun companion, quick to learn the fashioning of a sushi roll much faster than he, but neither mocking him for his clumsy fingers nor deriding him for his lack of knowledge about anything Japanese. In fact, he'd embraced every moment of her lively presence, and the lesson passed on swift wings.

To his surprise, upon his arrival he had discovered a kitchen crowded with eager participants for this first demonstration of Japanese cuisine, and Pixie had told him that Tessa had a waiting list for the next round of three-week lessons.

Mr Fukuka was a patient and informative teacher who made the first lesson easy. When the session had finished, everyone gave him a resounding cheer before they gathered their plates and wandered into the formal dining room, where they shared the food they had prepared during the class.

There was a lot of laughter and chatter afterwards until the participants began gathering up their coats, scarves and handbags, giving their thanks before departing for home. Abby and Roman Taylor left with Ernest Callen and Dr Fatima as they had shared transport to the Lodge. Natalie and Troy Davidson soon left on the heels of Leslie Wolski.

Voices sounded in the foyer, and Jordan glanced up as Billie and Kirk strolled into the room, sporting big grins and with Pastor Miller on their heels.

His gut tightened like a screw.

"Hello, everyone. We've got some news to share." Billie shot Kirk a quick look, then when he nodded, burst out with, "We're having a baby!"

They were swarmed by family, Tessa with tears of joy streaming down her cheeks, her daughters yelling with excitement while Ms Lette demanded to know how long Florrie had been keeping this secret from her. Jordan held back as Dodge slapped Kirk's back and gave him a man hug. And then Mrs Brown and the Fukuka's surged forward to offer their congrats.

A warm hand slipped into his, gripping firm for a few precious seconds, and then Pixie left his side, pouncing on her brother and Billie, flinging her arms around their necks and squealing with delight.

Jordan offered a more restrained congratulation to them both, restricting himself to a handshake with Kirk and a quick peck on Billie's cheek.

Ms Lette ordered champagne to be brought forward, but Billie negated that suggestion. So, they settled for a fresh pot of tea, which they drank while sitting around the formal dining table. After everyone had settled down and finished with their million questions and exclamations, Mrs Brown rose, announcing it was time for them to leave. Dodge then drove Mr and Mrs Fukuka and Mrs Brown home while Tessa shooed her two daughters to their rooms, leaving Jordan in the dining room with the happy couple, Pastor Miller, Ms Lette and Pixie.

Kirk moved to the sideboard and brought out a bottle of Shiraz. "Anyone like a drink before getting down to business?"

Jordan declined, knowing he had a long winding road on the return trip to the farm, and settled back. Everyone else shook their heads, so Kirk poured himself a small glass while Billie produced a tablet, and her mother nattered about the wedding menu. Whatever Jordan thought they'd be discussing that night - it hadn't been food, and as the minutes ticked by, he couldn't figure out why it had been considered essential for him to be present. Unless it had been intended that he hear the news about the baby.

As if she had guessed his thoughts, Billie glanced over and met Jordan's eyes.

There was a question lurking there, and he sensed that she needed to know he was okay with this news.

And he discovered that he was.

He smiled.

Relief seeped the last tension from his body when she nodded back.

He knew immediately their relationship was back on the same steady ground it had held when they were kids.

Best mates.

With a half glass of red, Kirk resumed his seat, and the chat about hors d'oeuvres grew louder.

Rubbing his eyes where a headache had bloomed, Jordan muttered how he was heading to the kitchen and left the room, with Ms Lette calling after him to help himself to whatever he wanted. He was standing by the sink, staring out the window at the darkness shrouding the rear yard and slowly sipping a glass of cold water when he tensed. Although he hadn't heard Pixie's footsteps, there was no mistaking the faint tantalising scent of apples that seemed to cling to her soft-looking hair. Or the instinctive thrum that erupted deep inside his body whenever she was near.

"You okay, babe?"

Breath catching in his throat, he glanced down at where she'd placed a gentle hand on his forearm, the note of concern in her voice tugging on his heartstrings. But was it real? Or was it like everything she manufactured for her social media sites, a sham? A juiced-up, glitzy, romanticised fantasy that had little connection to the ordinary, everyday kind of world he inhabited.

"I'm fine," he said abruptly.

Wanting her to leave.

Wanting her to stay.

Wanting, he wasn't sure what.

She huffed out a breath and moved to stand beside him.

Instantly, he missed her touch.

"I'm happy for my bro, but...it's hard too. Once upon a time, I wanted what he has, love, a wedding, and all that happy-ever-after guff."

Setting down the glass, he turned, leaning back against the sink. "My mother always says it's never too late."

"Hey, I'm not saying I don't love my life. I do. I get the remote all to myself, have no one to answer to, and do what I want – all the time."

He quirked an eyebrow. "Sure, that doesn't scream – loneliness?"

Her eyes narrowed. "Hmm. You should talk. Aren't you single, too?"

"Yep. Single. Live at home with my parents. That's me. Although at least I'm not under the same roof anymore. I built a separate grannie flat for myself a few years ago, but I still share my meals with my parents. Gives me an excuse to keep an eye on their health."

Pushing away from the sink, he crossed to the refrigerator and said over his shoulder, "I'm making hot choco-late. Want one?"

"With marshmallows?"

"No idea if there's any. But it does sound tempting."

"I'll look." Humming under her breath, she opened the cupboards while he located the milk, the cocoa and a cooking pot.

A few minutes later, he poured the hot chocolate into a couple of mugs while Pixie gleefully popped two pink marshmallows in each. Before taking his drink, he cleaned up the little mess he had made while she stored away the milk and the marshmallow packet.

"We make a good team," she said, then sent him a mischievous look, which he did his best to ignore, blowing on his drink before taking a cautious sip.

Cupping her hands around her own mug, Pixie stared into its depths. "I'm not sure I can handle any more of that conversation about mini quiches or pate sandwiches."

"Yeah. I figured my opinion on the wedding menu isn't particularly relevant – hence my escape to the kitchen."

"Same." She met his eyes. "There's a fire burning in the library. We could take our drinks there and chill."

Smiling, he raised his mug and toasted her. "Good plan. Lead on, MacDuff."

Chuckling softly, she led the way through the old house and ushered him into a room where he instantly felt at home.

"Wow. I never knew Ms Lette had a real old-fashioned library room in her house. Some of these issues look like first editions." Gazing with appreciation, he strolled around, admiring the well-polished timber bookcases lining the walls, the comfy sofas, strategically placed floor lamps and the fluffy hearth rug sprawled before the fireplace, where as promised, a fire crackled and glowed.

"Now this, I like."

"I know. Isn't it wonderful? Reading is up there on my favourite pastimes." Mug in one hand, Pixie trailed her scarlet-painted fingertips along the spines of a row of books.

"Really?" Jordan looked at her, taking in the whimsical smile lurking about her full lips.

"Yes. Really. I can read, you know." She threw him a mock glare.

He raised a hand in surrender, his lips quirking. "I apologise for thinking your life relies totally on social media."

"I have beauty as well as brains." She tapped her forehead.

"And modesty, too."

They looked at each other and laughed.

Feeling more relaxed than he'd ever felt before in a woman's presence, Jordan patted the back of the sofa. "Care to sit for a while?"

"Thought you'd never ask."

She whisked herself over, and they settled down, side by side, on the comfortable couch. Leaning her head back against the rear cushion, she sighed. "Oh, this is nice."

"Yeah, it's just about perfect." He didn't dare glance at her again. She was so close if he shifted just a tad more to his right, they'd be pressing against each other.

His pulse hiccupped and then surged into a stampede, but he didn't move. Instead, he imitated her, snuggling further into the cushions and sipping his hot drink. Simply being there with her right now was enough.

"Name your favourite genre."

She peeped at him over the rim of her mug. "Don't judge. It's science fiction, preferably space opera."

"No kidding?" Mouth agape, he stared at her.

"Favourite author?" he croaked.

"C J Thorpe," she said promptly.

Then, when he stared at her, she added, "What did I say? I know – don't tell me, that's your favourite genre and author too!"

He shook his head. "Nope. Not even close. Well, kinda."

Taking a steadying breath, all the while wondering what she'd make of what he intended to divulge, he said, "That's me. I'm C J Thorpe."

"No!"

Now it was her turn to goggle at him.

"Seriously?" she squealed, almost sloshing her hot chocolate all over herself and the sofa as she snapped upright.

"You're him? OMGosh! I thought you were a farmer!"

"I am. Growing up, I always dabbled in writing short stories for my own amusement, but we hit a difficult patch about eleven years ago. Thought we'd lose the farm, lose everything, actually. I decided I had nothing to lose, so I wrote a story that had been playing inside my head for a while. I sent it to several publishers and agents and was rejected everywhere. But this one publisher offered suggestions and said they'd be prepared to revisit my submission if I took their comments on board and made significant revisions. I packed away my ego and knuckled down. And they did better than taking another look at my work. I was offered a contract."

"What does the 'C. J.' stand for?"

"My dog is called CJ."

"Awww, that is so sweet! I can't believe I'm sitting next to the C J Thorpe!" she all but shouted.

"Please keep your voice down."

"What? Don't tell me no one else knows?"

"Only my parents and sisters."

She blinked at him slowly, then smiled. "And now me."

He wagged a finger at her. "I hope you will keep this between us."

"You can trust me, Jordan." Her voice was firm, her gaze steady as she ate him up with those glorious eyes of hers. She held out her free hand.

"I know I can."

Feeling as if something momentous had changed between them, he reached out and their fingers locked together.

"I'll tell you something that I've never shared on social media, I love going to the sci-fi conventions."

"Same. I went to one in Las Vegas a few years ago and had an absolute ball."

"Maybe we could go together sometime," she said slowly.

"Maybe," he whispered, mesmerised by the warmth of her expression.

Footsteps sounded on the hardwood floor, and the next instant, Tessa said from the doorway, "Hey, sorry to interrupt, but everyone is calling it a night."

Her brown eyes, bright with inquisitiveness, widened as she spotted them sitting on the couch, hand in hand. "I'll see you next time, Jordan. Pixie, catch you in the morning. I'm off to bed."

Covering her yawn, she quickly retreated, but not before Jordan heard her quiet snigger.

Slipping his hand free from Pixie's, Jordan drained his mug. "That's my cue."

"Don't worry about washing the mugs; I will see to it."

"Thanks, I appreciate that."

He hesitated, then clamped his mouth tight over words he wouldn't, no, couldn't say. They may have shared a moment just then, but when he faced the facts, there was no future with a woman who lived on the other side of the world. It was dumb of him to even entertain the smallest of fantasies. At least, that was the stern warning he administered to himself as he marched through the house, far too aware of her presence so close behind him.

Tongue-tied, his stomach in knots, he pulled on the boots he'd left on the front veranda.

Straightening, he dithered beneath the glare of the overhead light as tension fizzed between them.

She stared back at him like she was waiting for something until she stepped backwards with a faint sigh.

"See you soon, babe."

She tossed him her trademark cheeky smile, accompanied by a wink that sent all his blood south and spun his head in a whirl as she closed the door.

Hands thrust deep into his jeans pockets, he stepped out into the night, unable to stop the grin tugging at his lips. The realisation sank deep that he was looking forward to their next encounter, although the bitter knowledge she could never be his was like a blight upon his soul.

Chapter Seven

Gut churning, Jordan parked up out front of the CWA hall and killed the engine, waiting a few seconds before reaching for the keys. With his dual cab ute now turned off, the warmth generated by the big car's heater quickly withered in the face of the chilly autumn day. Up ahead, an elderly couple wrapped up in puffy coats and beanies plodded forward, one pushing a walker, no doubt heading for the local supermarket.

There were few cars in the street. The parking lot to the side of the hall was empty, although the door stood open, indicating someone had turned up to unlock it. Probably, they had already hightailed it home to spend the day in front of a fire. A light wind scattered fallen leaves along the footpath and over the hall's front steps while the heavy clouds overhead hung low and dark with the threat of more rain.

He drummed his fingers on the steering wheel without looking at where his mother sat far too tense in the passenger seat.

"You sure about this?"

Hilary snorted. "What's to be sure about? I'm looking forward to it, to be honest. Especially since neither you nor your two sisters have shown any interest whatsoever in my baking skills."

"I'm a busy man," he defended himself.

Reaching out, his mother touched him gently on the cheek. "I know, son. I know."

Then she shot him a mischievous grin that wrung his heartstrings as he tried to recall the last time he saw that youthful expression on her face. The past few years had been difficult for all of them, but more so for his mum.

"The truth is, you're a terrible cook."

"Hey! My bangers and mash are legendary."

"Keep telling yourself that, son. Maybe someone will eventually believe you." Hilary snickered, then with her hand on the handle, she hesitated, biting her lower lip.

"What if no one turns up? After all, learning how to make and decorate gingerbread houses may not be very popular these days. And I can't see any other cars."

"We had to be here early, remember? To set every-thing up?" His voice was gentle. "Come on. Let's get this show on the road."

Stepping out of the car, he moved to the rear tray and

hefted out a filled-to-the-brim cardboard box, glad to see his mother had found her game face and was already trotting towards the hall. Still, he had worried over the same question when Mrs Brown phoned a couple of weeks ago and all but ordered his mother to put her hand up and volunteer. Sure, there had been a lot of flattery involved about how his mum made the best gingerbread ever, etcetera, etcetera. Which was quite true. But still…

Cooking classes.

Did anyone even cook for themselves anymore? Wasn't it all frozen meals and takeaways?

But Jordan had to admit, he'd been surprised at the number of people who had attended the Japanese class the previous night, so maybe he was more out of touch than he realised. Hopefully, his mum would have a similar result. With his two younger sisters off pursuing their lives far from the family farm, it had been up to Jordan to support his mother when she pleaded for help. And now here he was – her official assistant.

But he wouldn't be alone.

His pulse fired on all neurons, pulsing his blood far too fast and hot for comfort.

Pixie. The other assistant.

He sighed, shifting the box in his arms a trifle as he turned around.

Exactly how that American woman had become involved with the class his mother was running was a complete mystery.

As if his thoughts had conjured her out of thin air,

she popped up beside him, a far too pretty genie with ruffled dark brown hair and a fluffy red scarf wound around her neck.

"Let me help with that."

She went to wrest the heavy box from his arms.

"It's fine. Leave it," Jordan growled, trying to do a sidestep to avoid smacking into her.

But to his horror, his left foot went down a hole (probably dug by some pesky possum), the weight in the box shifted, and he lost his balance.

"I've got you!" she shouted, grabbing his arm and yanking him in the opposite direction.

He balled, "Crap!"

And over they went in a tangle of limbs, jars, bottles of spices and full Tupperware containers.

A kookaburra burst into its signature cackling laugh from a nearby gum tree.

Perfect timing.

For two long beats of his heart, Jordan remained where he lay, aware of only two things; the fragrant apple scent of her hair shampoo and the softness of her body as he sprawled on top of her.

"I can't breathe," she said in a hoarse voice.

Wanting to crawl down the same blasted hole that had caused this debacle in the first place, Jordan mumbled, "Sorry."

And rolled off her, leaping to his feet like they were on fire.

"All good."

She sounded breathless.

He didn't dare glance at her, even though the urge to do so was almost like a physical force dragging him to a place he refused to go. Ducking his head to hide the flush in his cheeks, he swooped down and shoved the scattered items back into the box.

Thankfully, she kept her distance this time.

"Anything else I need to bring inside?"

"Yeah. There's a smaller box but leave the esky, I'll get that. It's too heavy for you."

"I'm not a lightweight."

She sounded so irritated that he had to look.

Her hands were on her hips, her head held high, but damn, there was a cute smirk tugging at her lips that made him want to...

"Jordan! Is everything alright? What happened here?"

And there was his mother hurrying down the steps, face creased into anxious lines, hands outstretched.

"All good, Mum. Just didn't see where I was going."

"I'm sorry, it was me. I accidentally sent Jordan flying."

Pixie spoke at the same time as him. Both rushed their explanation, both avoiding looking at each other.

"Oh?"

That one word was loaded with far too many questions and sent Jordan's eyes rolling back so far that they could have hit the rear of his skull.

He darted a quick glance at Pixie and then his mother as she advanced towards them, smiling.

"I'm Hilary. And you must be Kirk's sister. How lovely to meet you."

"Pixie Wellington, the pleasure is mine."

They shook hands and walked into the hall, chatting, leaving Jordan to take all the boxes as well as the esky inside.

He found them busily setting up a long trestle table that had been placed near the stage area. He dumped the box down, trudged out the hall and brought in the rest of the gear.

"What do you want me to do now?"

"Is there a whiteboard of some description?" Pixie turned to his mother. "It might be a good idea for you to write the important points on the board; it is easier for people to see even though they'll have a copy of your handouts."

Hilary nodded. "I like that idea, but my handwriting is atrocious. Perhaps you could do it for me, Pixie, if I tell you what to write?"

"I'm all over it."

"I'll locate the whiteboard, should be in the storage room." With a tight smile, Jordan strode off towards a badly painted beige door.

The three of them worked together for the next twenty minutes, readying everything for the class until his mother was as satisfied with their efforts as she could be. Thankfully, the frigidness of the room was beginning to lessen courtesy of the wall heaters Jordan had turned on after he'd finished positioning the folding chairs. Several trestle tables had been assembled, giving the participants sufficient space to prepare their gingerbread dough and have a notebook or tablet in easy reach.

Hilary twitched the small desk easel on which she'd printed out an image of a small town made entirely of gingerbread, a centimetre to the left, then clasped her hands together, frowning as she looked towards the door.

"Five minutes until start time. I can't believe I agreed to do this – and I will have to keep doing it until the end of July. I'm no teacher."

Jordan guffawed. "A few minutes ago, you said you had this in the bag. Seriously, no need to worry, Mum, you'll be fine."

He squeezed her shoulder. "Listen, there's voices outside."

Pixie, who had been filming the whiteboard and the laden front table and for once not yakking away incessantly, surged into motion. The woman never seemed to be still for longer than five minutes.

"I'll round them up." She winked, then sashayed to the door, long legs outlined in figure-hugging jeans.

Yeah.

She really did sashay, swinging her hips like she knew he had his eyes glued to her butt.

His mother elbow nudged him and whispered, "I like her."

Pretending he hadn't heard, he fidgeted with the

printouts, re-aligning the edges as Pixie ushered the first participants, welcoming them in her clear voice with its distinctive American accent that rang through the hall.

"Hey, Jordan. Good to see you, mate."

To his surprise, he looked up to see Mark Altman, who he'd met a few years ago after the bloke had asked his permission to check out his farm for some rare plant or other, and since then, met up occasionally at the pub. Strolling next to him with her hand in his was his partner, Leah.

"You here for the gingerbread classes?" Jordan's voice held more than a little hint of surprise.

"Leah wants to totally embrace the town's first Christmas in July." Mark grinned. "What about you?"

"I'm Mum's little helper."

"Good on you, mate." Mark sniggered as he clapped a hand on Jordan's back.

"Catch up with you soon?"

Mark nodded. "I'll text."

"Great."

They moved away to choose their seats.

"Friends of yours?" came the breathy enquiry from Pixie, hovering far too close to his side.

Hadn't the woman heard of personal space?

"Yeah, we're on the same trivia team at the local pub."

Beside him, his mother checked her watch, gave an audible gulp, then, picking up a tiny bell, rang it several times.

The general hubbub in the hall quietened, and he realised that as he'd been chatting, most people had chosen their tables and seats. There was a bit of a stir at the entrance, and he bit back his groan when Ms Lette stalked into the hall, wearing her trademark gumboots and leading what looked like a veritable pack of women.

All looking at him.

All sharing smiling glances with each other. Like they knew something Jordan didn't. It was downright uncomfortable, and he had to resist the need to shuffle his feet and slink out of sight.

"Edwina!" called his mother, a sure invitation for the old woman to come closer and chat. Not that Ms Edwina Lette ever needed an invitation to do anything. She was known throughout the length and breadth of Bindarra Creek as being a force to be reckoned with. Alongside her was one of her besties, Billie's mum, who grinned happily at Jordan. Meanwhile, flanking Ms Lette's other side like a destroyer surging beside an aircraft carrier was Mrs Pamela Brown with her sister trailing behind.

Jordan shuddered as the mob fetched up in front of the main table.

"Everything looks in order." Mrs Brown scowled and swept the hall with her sharp gaze like an army sergeant inspecting the barracks.

His mother gave a nervous cough. "I hope so."

"Humph," snorted Mrs Brown.

Her sister, Mrs Fukuka, smiled gently. "I'm looking forward to making my first gingerbread house. Of course,

Pam and I have made cookies before, but never anything as challenging as a house."

"I won't hold you up. I'm not staying, I have a fortune-telling appointment in five." Ms Lette winked, and for some reason, Jordan's face heated.

The two sisters and Mrs Miller moved off to snag the last vacant table.

Ms Lette slapped the pockets of her purple hoodie as if searching for something. Then, she appeared to give up, half turning to tug a younger woman to the fore. "Brought someone with me. This is Lena. I remembered last night that she hosted a gingerbread house decorating party a couple of years ago and thought she may be useful."

Lena said as her glance darted between them, "Hey there. Hope I'm not intruding."

"Oh no, dear. Of course not." Hilary beamed before adding uncertainly, "Thank you for agreeing to help. Jordan here can only cook sausages, but I'm not certain of Pixie's skills. No disrespect intended, dear."

Pixie laughed, reaching across the table with her hand outstretched, and they shook hands. "Is that an American accent I hear? That is magic! We must have coffee. And please, Hilary, I don't blame you for being wary. Cookies I can do, but moulding and decorating a house out of dough? I can't wait to learn such a fascinating skill."

Lena smiled at Hilary as she produced sheets of printed paper from her bag. "I hope you don't mind, but

I come bearing gifts. This is my great-grandmother's gingerbread cookie recipe. Maybe you could offer it as a bonus?"

"How wonderful!" Hilary took the offered sheets. "This will be a wonderful surprise for everyone. Is it okay with you if we leave it as a surprise announcement on the last day of our workshop?"

"Works for me." Lena looked at Pixie, pulled out a band, and tied her long dark hair into a tail. "You're that influencer everyone in town has been talking about, aren't you?"

Pixie squealed and turned to Jordan, giving him a mock punch on the arm. "See, babe? I told you I'm famous. Yes, I surely am she. About that coffee?"

"Love to. Let's swap numbers after the lesson."

"It's three minutes past starting time," bawled Mrs Brown from across the room.

Hilary blushed, knocked on the table, and then began to welcome the participants in a loud voice. In a whirl of energy, Pixie shoved half of the paper stack at Jordan and bustled off to hand them out; and Jordan quickly followed. Lena moved to sit beside Hilary, murmuring a few suggestions whenever Hilary hesitated as if she'd forgotten what she intended to say.

And the workshop began.

His mother had always believed the way to learn any new skill was to do the thing yourself. She had been that way all through Jordan and his sisters' childhoods, there to lend a hand but insistent they try things for themselves. Whether it was tying their own shoelaces at the age of three, cleaning their rooms when they were six or making their own decisions when they were eighteen. She was no different running a cooking demonstration, and it wasn't long before everyone was elbow-deep in flour, and the rich tang of spices filled the air.

"Do you think it's going okay?" Hilary whispered.

The atmosphere in the hall hummed with infectious energy and bustle, and it was obvious everyone was having a good time.

"It's going great, Mum." Jordan smiled, and he wasn't the only one who noticed the change in her demeanour, his chest swelling as both Pixie and Lena warmly appreciated her efforts by calling out *'Good job'*.

Turning, his hungry gaze ate up the sight of Pixie's beaming face and the way her sparkling eyes glowed with pleasure as she watched his mother.

And then, as if sensing his regard, she faced him.

And her warm and wonderful expression all but felled him where he stood.

Chapter Eight

"Your mom is a fabulous cook and teacher. I wonder if she would consider teaching other classes on a regular basis?" Pixie mused as she pushed strands of hair out of her eyes.

"You've got..." He brushed his knuckles over her cheeks, and it was as if a trail of fire seared across her skin.

"Oh, thanks." Heat bloomed where he had touched her, and she couldn't stop her smirk from growing, noticing how his gaze remained on her as if he was mesmerised.

Her breathing shortened as her pulse raced, sending hot blood coursing like a flooding river through her veins. She could have stood there staring at Jordan forever, wallowing in the reassuring strength of his aura, the honesty in his gaze. Was it real, or was he putting his best face forward for the sake of his mother and her class? She wondered what he would do if she wrapped her arms around his neck and kissed him. To see what he tasted like, to see if he tasted – real. Suddenly, the need to do just that caused her to sway forward. Her lips parted; she gulped, and her fingers and other parts she didn't want to think about tingled.

Someone emitted a shriek of surprise elsewhere inside the hall. Dragged back to reality, she stared at the table, hoping no one had noticed, aware that her knees had gone all mushy on her like she was standing on two marshmallows instead of flesh and bone.

"Your mom?" she prompted when the silence between them had gone on for too long, and she finally remembered what she had asked him.

Face fierce, he dug his hands into the bowl and attempted to scoop the sticky mixture into a mound, but the dough stuck to the sides of the bowl and his hands. "No idea. Guess you'll have to check with her yourself."

"Don't worry, I will."

"You like being busy?"

"Gosh, yes. Busy bee, that's me."

Even she caught the note of faint bitterness in her tone.

Frowning, he sent her a searching stare that she met with a limpid glance before she produced her mobile and began to record herself speaking about the class. Yeah, yeah, a way too obvious deflection act, but she didn't trust herself to not spill her most secret misgivings about herself. To prove to both Jordan and her she was on top of it all, she spent the next several minutes strolling about the hall, chatting to people while filming.

Unable to stay away from him for too long, Pixie reappeared by his side. She placed her phone onto a mini easel, checked the red recording light was on and then dusted a tad more flour over her dough before rolling the mixture around the bowl. She rose to her tiptoes, then back to the floor, then back up again as she gently patted the dough into an oblong shape.

"I meant to tell you earlier, then forgot. Tessa has asked me to check with you about the Lette float. Are you still on board with providing the truck? We could also use another guy who can wield a hammer. Kirk is hopeless, which means poor Dodge will have to bear the brunt of the work making the set, so another pair of hands would be awesome."

Pausing for breath, she leaned over to peer into his bowl.

"Ugh, what is that?"

Jordan's fingers stilled where they were dug deep in a soggy mixture that looked nothing like the smooth dough that resided in Pixie's own bowl. He looked at her and then back to his pitiful efforts, emitting such a woe-be-gone sigh that she couldn't help but giggle. Flour clung in mushy clumps to his fingers while a few lumps plopped from his hands back into the bowl.

"This doesn't look so good," he muttered.

Pixie chuckled again.

"Tell me something I don't know! You've got way too much moisture there, babe. Add some more flour."

He frowned. "Eh. Won't that dilute the ginger taste?"

"Hmm, good point." She looked about the hall.

Hilary had been working the room for the past five minutes and was now situated at the back, guiding several older women who appeared to be doing more talking than mixing. Shawn and his partner, Leslie, who Pixie had met several times now and knew by sight, hovered next to Hilary, holding a bowl and probably waiting for her to finish so she could help them as well.

Pixie waved Lena over from where the other woman had been helping a group of giggling late teens, a few of whom she recognised; Drew Taylor there was no mistaking that orange-red hair of his, his buddy, Ethan Beasley and Tessa's daughter Kaylee. The Maloof girls were also present and currently flicking blobs of dough at each other while their mother, Dr Fatima, and her husband, the archaeologist Ernest Callen, were mixing up multiple mounds of dough as if they intended to build an entire new civilisation. A hoot of laughter erupted from the side where Abby and Roman Taylor, AJ, and Troy Davidson were rolling out their dough as if having a mini contest to see who could do it the fastest.

For some odd reason, the knowledge of how many of these people she now knew warmed her from her toes to the top of her head. And she didn't just know their names, several were well on the way to becoming firm friends.

"Oh boy," said Lena as she appeared and inspected Jordan's work. Her face worked as if she was holding back a grin.

"Make up a new mixture but ensure its dryer than what you have here; then gently knead this one into it, and hopefully, that will make a firmer dough. It can't be too wet, but it can't be too dry either. I don't think it will matter if you end up with a larger amount. Maybe you could make another gingerbread house or just make it bigger? That way, you won't waste any of the dough."

"How about a kangaroo? I'd love a gingerbread kangaroo." Pixie turned to Jordan, as she added a long, drawn out, "Pleeeeaaaassssse, babe. You'll be way better at making a kangaroo than I would be."

"I do have a name, you know."

He was such a grump. She just loved teasing him.

"And it's a lovely name, babe. Now - a kangaroo?"

Jordan rolled his eyes. "Right. A kangaroo. No pressure. I can barely make a round biscuit!"

"You'll do just fine." Pixie giggled, wrapping a floury hand around his forearm and squeezing, instantly feeling how he tensed at her touch. It was enough to give a girl goosebumps. Not to mention energising a very pleasing fantasy!

His Adam's apple bobbed, and she hid a satisfied grin.

"Someone else needs me. Good luck, you two." Lena

nodded to them and moved off to help a young woman with a toddler seated beside her and who was beckoning frantically.

"About the float?" she prompted, breathing in the woody scent of his aftershave and feeling just that little bit dizzy. He always smelt so clean and fresh!

"Guess I could lend a hand with the float."

"You're such a hero." She fluttered her long black lashes in his direction, noting that he stared at them like he'd never seen such long lashes before. They were fake, of course, but they were the best kind of fake. The way Jordan stared at her as if he never wanted to wrench his gaze away made her pleased that she had spent so much care on her appearance that morning.

Ducking his head, he poured cups of flour into the bowl, adding enough ginger to cure the common cold and more spices. He pounded his gooey mess onto the counter like he was going several rounds in a boxing ring, giving the mound one last knuckle thump for good measure, while Pixie filmed him, aware that she was probably annoying him like mad. And for some reason, that made her want to laugh and tease him even more.

He mumbled, "Most Sundays should work for me if that's good for you and the others?"

"Great plan. That should fit in with everyone's work schedules just fine."

"When do you need the truck?"

"As soon as - if that's okay? That way, we can build

the set straight onto the truck without having to shift it later. Unless you think you may need the truck before the parade?"

"Pretty sure I don't need it any time soon."

He shrugged as he clapped his hands as if hoping to rid himself of the sticky mess, but it only worsened the goo coating his hands.

"Here, let me."

Pixie replaced her phone on the easel, then produced a tea towel and began scrapping the mixture off his hands and onto the table.

From the rear came Hilary's raised voice.

"Excuse me, everyone. Quiet, please."

Pixie wadded up the towel and elbow-nudged Jordan.

Once the bubble of babble faded, Hilary continued. "Now, I know you are all very eager to make your houses, but...unfortunately, your dough must be refrigerated for a few hours before rolling out into the necessary shapes before going into the oven to bake. When you're doing this at home, remember refrigerating your dough overnight will give you the best results. Since the class is held only one day a week, we'll need to wait until next time for the cooking process."

A collective mock groan rolled around the hall as Hilary trotted to the main table.

With the end of her rolling pin, she indicated the points on the whiteboard. "Let's go through the main points - it's important that you follow the steps as laid out in your sheets. Now, it's almost time for our session to close for the day. I want everyone to wrap their dough in the clingwrap provided here on this table, making sure that it is airtight. Use a black marker to label it with your name, then store it in the refrigerator through that door to your right. Next week, we will roll the dough into shapes, and bake them, while on the following week we will begin to assemble our houses."

The room erupted into movement, and Pixie switched off her filming, stowing her phone into her handbag, then looked at the mess on the tables they had to clear up. At least a good hour's work lay before them before they could leave.

"One more thing – actually, two more things," Hilary called.

"Your homework. I want everyone to work on their design and decide how and what you will use to decorate your houses. In the handouts, you will find as many suggestions as possible that I could think of, along with my contact details. Please feel free to reach out if you have any questions. Lastly, thank you all for coming here today."

A round of applause thundered through the hall, and Pixie joined in, clapping so hard that her hands hurt.

"She's really something," muttered Jordan.

Pixie nodded. "Yeah, she sure is a special kind of lady."

He turned and smiled at her.

Her heart fluttered as if it had wings, her legs wobbling like melting jelly; Pixie gripped the table edge hard. Hilary wasn't the only one who was special.

Chapter Nine

The weeks raced past, blurring together like tumbleweeds rolling along in the wind as the Christmas in July festival drew ever closer and the town buzzed with activity. Pixie rose to greet the day every morning by experiencing the dawn, something she had rarely done. She spent a delicious hour alone on the top veranda outside her bedroom door, wrapped in a thick doona, fluffy socks on her feet, and simply listening and watching as nature awoke. She could even now identify a few of the native birds: the distinctive kookaburra, which always made her smile, and the difference between the melodious songs of the magpie and the silver-backed butcherbird. Occasionally (but that was becoming rarer), she would go over her plans for that day, what posts she intended to upload to her social media sites, check the status and comments from the previous day, and analyse the overall engagement relevance of her posts. Gradually, her reluctance to visit the digital world she'd created grew stronger. But every single day, as the birds filled the air with their morning warbles and chatter, and the wisps of fog floated through tree branches like snippets of memories, her thoughts would return over and over to what was rapidly becoming a compulsively fascinating subject – Jordan.

And what – if anything – did she intend to do about the strengthening of her feelings towards him.

The safest course was to steer clear and avoid him completely. That was doable; Pixie did have a few options in that regard. One - was to hightail it back to the States and the familiarity of her old life, which had never offered as many emotional challenges as this small town seemed to do; second – she could hoist all these festival responsibilities she'd absorbed onto someone else's shoulders which would then limit their contact. She could cite the necessity to concentrate on her business. A lack of interest, care, boredom – although she suspected not one person here would believe a word of any of that since she had embraced this life with such enthusiasm.

But whenever the thought of severing whatever it was that lay between her and Jordan entered her head, a deep sense of loss and emptiness would swamp her.

When it came down to bare bones, he had captured more than her thoughts. But was her attraction a simple holiday infatuation? Something insanely intense but fleeting that would never strengthen and weather the challenges of reality?

Nowhere in her plans, her hopes, her dreams did a long-term relationship with a farmer who lived in a small town on the opposite side of the world fit. She had formulated her ambitions many years ago and never factored in love. And she had wanted – no needed – to succeed for so long; it was like a drug in her system, an addiction she doubted she could shake.

Still, there was no denying how much she enjoyed Jordan's company; he was fun, interesting, and intelligent, and she just loved listening to his accent and prying open his opinions on every subject possible. However, all those wonderful, warm, cosy feelings his conversations engendered were nothing compared to the thrill of his physical presence. How her knees quivered, and her belly turned to jelly at his touch. How much she yearned to feel his lips on hers.

But that was a line she refused to cross no matter how she ached for his caress, instinctively acknowledging that once crossed, she, for one, could never go back. She would want more.

And how could such a liaison figure into her plans?

As May became June and then surged into July, she hugged her times spent with Jordan close, like a child with a beloved stuffed toy who feared one more wash would mean its disintegration.

Her status as an influencer was growing exponentially; she seemed to hit all the right notes with her followers, and their likes and shares brought even more fans to her sites. She couldn't help but feel proud of her achievements, even more so when she shared the latest stats with Jordan, and he congratulated her. She knew he wasn't keen on social media, which made his sincere interest in her achievements priceless.

Also surprising was that the new friends she had made in this small town made a point of both liking her posts and bringing her work into their conversations. It made her feel as if her work was valued, which had not happened for a long time.

Then there had been that special moment at the surprise baby shower Tessa had organised for Billie, held in the vicarage garden. The day had been sunny and clear, if a little cool. A light breeze, bringing the scent of jasmine, whispered through the pergola where they sat in chairs or on brightly coloured cushions on a massive rug. After Billie had unwrapped the gifts and they had been ooohed and ahhhed over by Billie, Pastor Millers and all the other women who were present, Tessa poured everyone a fresh glass of homemade lemonade (no alcohol due to Billie's condition!). She then spoke about Billie, the wedding, the baby that would soon arrive and how much it would be loved.

Everyone cheered, and Pixie's eyes pricked with unshed tears. Glancing around at these women of varying ages who had all become rather special to her, she realised she wasn't the only one affected.

"I also would like to add one more thing. Everyone, if

you could raise your glasses again?" Tessa beamed around the group, and then her gaze settled on Pixie.

"First, I just want to say how lovely it's been to get to know you better, Pixie, and more importantly, how very grateful I am for the help you have given me, our family and this town. Your time, your energy and your amazing enthusiasm have lifted me up on days when I was feeling overwhelmed. I'm proud to announce that all the accommodation in town has been booked out for the festival, including the Lodge; the town is bulging with tourists, and every event has been booked out. We have a fabulous number of people who have entered the Lucky Door Farm weekend prize, and I'm certain that the success of our Christmas in July festival will be mostly due to Pixie's social media skills. So thank you, Pixie. You're a legend, and I'm so happy to call you my friend!"

And that's when Pixie did cry.

***

One of the many glorious memories attained over the past weeks that Jordan continually examined and scrutinised as if he were a scientist probing for the origin of life was the few hours when he and Pixie dragged themselves away from the Lette family float to attend a couple of the Christmas movies. The movies were special screenings that were run on most July weekends. Apart from their shared passion for science fiction, they also discovered a love of kids' movies and buttered popcorn, laughing through the first sessions, which showcased *Home Alone* on Saturday, followed by *Home Alone 2* the next day. Then there were the gingerbread cooking classes they attended together every Saturday morning. And, of course, the Japanese classes on Friday nights, after which there were Billie's wedding details to be sorted through, culminating in the highlight (for him that was) in more alone time spent with Pixie in the Lodge's library where they sipped hot chocolate and talked about everything and anything.

Never had he felt such a strong connection with another person. She was like the best mate rolled into an amusing, stimulating and downright sexy woman whose smile was like sunshine brightening every day.

The knowledge that she was only here until after her brother's wedding and then she'd be gone – probably forever – hung over his head like an executioner's sword.

But whatever dark future lay before him, he was determined to make the most of every moment.

That included the days when they worked on the Lette float together, which led him to today when she was there to assist him with his truck. He was positive he'd heard the engine misfire when he'd driven it into town before parking it in a spare shed on Fred's Garage lot. No way he could have the vehicle breaking down in the middle of the parade, so he'd marked out a few hours to give it an overhaul.

They had spent the Sunday morning with Tessa and Dodge toiling over the display, but after a packed lunch that Dodge had supplied, Jordan decided now was the time to check out the truck. Calling out cheery goodbyes and trying but failing to hide their knowing smirks, Tessa and Dodge returned home to spend the afternoon with their daughters, leaving Jordan and Pixie alone. After donning a pair of overalls, he dragged out his toolbox and asked Pixie to man the driver's seat. He popped his head under the bonnet and called her to rev the accelerator, frowning as his ears caught an intermittent stutter underlying the truck's rumble.

"Okay! Ease off, please."

The noise died, and, using a rag to protect his hands from the hot engine, he shifted aside a couple of hoses and peered closer, deciding the problem came from a dirty fuel line. Well, he could fix that issue, but it would take a couple of hours, and daylight was already fading from the sky, exacerbated by the clouds that had begun to darken the sky while they were eating lunch.

"Look who's arrived early!"

The sound of the forced cheer in Kirk's unexpected voice had Jordan poking his head out to find him approaching, a fixed grin pasted on his face. Keeping pace beside him was an unfamiliar man, but something in both blokes' expressions sent dread coiling in Jordan's gut.

Jordan straightened, reaching for a clean rag to wipe his greasy hands as Pixie peered through the side window. It was as if he was watching a corny chic-lit film play out in front of his eyes.

As if he was a spectator to the end of his world.

Pixie scrambled from the truck cabin, but her back was to him. For a moment, as the two men continued walking along the length of the truck, Jordan could have sworn he heard her sharp intake of air and saw her body stiffen as if she braced herself for something unpleasant.

Then she walked forward.

"Chad! Great to see you."

The stranger, Chad, the wanker who had broken her heart, opened his arms, and to Jordan's horror, Pixie appeared to melt right in there. Squished up against the bloke's chest as he kissed her cheek.

He ground his teeth; white-hot rage and black despair roiled through his body, a chain reaction on the verge of an explosion. Hands fisted, he could do nothing but wait as Pixie disentangled herself and spun around.

Her face confounded him, and all his anger, all his pain vaporised like steam. Whatever Pixie felt, whatever she thought, she'd hidden. No sign of tears or excitement in her eyes that, were usually so expressive he'd often mused they were like gazing into the mirror of her soul. Her skin was smooth and blank, like a paper doll. The urge to protect and give her whatever support she needed supplanted his emotional tsunami.

If she wanted him, he'd be there.

Kirk introduced Chad to Jordan.

They nodded, each sizing the other up.

Leaning against the closed driver door, Pixie sent him a veiled glance before looking at Chad and giving a polite enquiry about his plane trip. The conversation that ensued was stilted, almost forced and hinting at words that were not being said.

But what were they?

Was he about to hear a declaration of renewed affection from Chad to Pixie? A plea to begin again?

That thought almost brought him to his knees, causing him to drop the rag he held and grab hold of the hard metal of the truck bonnet.

"Thought we'd show Chad what the town has to offer by attending Karaoke night next Friday. How about it, Pix? Are you up to singing your heart out at the Riverside Pub? I hear the grand prize is a romantic getaway for two at one of Stevie Ryan's Star cottages," said Kirk. "Billie and I intend to have a go."

Grabbing hold of Pixie's hand, Chad smiled easily. "Sounds great to me. We always did sing an amazing duet together. Remember when we performed Sonny and Cher's, *I've Got You, Babe,* at Phoebe's nineteenth birthday bash? We brought the house down."

"Fun times." Pixie turned to Jordan, raising her eyebrows. "How's your singing voice?"

An image of Pixie gazing into her ex's eyes and singing a love song together was like a bucketload of acid in his gut, eroding his former desire to offer her support. Trying not to gnash his teeth, he muttered, "Not happening. I've got work to do."

Kirk shot him a curious glance while Pixie almost

cooed, "Pity. Well, Chad, I guess it's just you and me. Catch you later, babe."

Slipping her arms through her brother's and Chad's elbows, Pixie looked over her shoulder at Jordan and gave him a wink. Then she propelled the two blokes into motion, and together, they sauntered out of the shed, melting into the gloomy afternoon shadows.

How long Jordan stood staring at the space where she'd once been, like he'd been transformed into a pillar of granite, he didn't know until the trilling of his mobile jerked him from his misery.

He recognised the call sign.

His father.

It was time he got back to a life and responsibilities that had nothing in common with a certain American woman.

Chapter Ten

"That was perfect," Pixie mumbled as she finished recording her first post of the morning. She had filmed herself having breakfast, a meal of scrambled free-range eggs, roasted tomatoes from the garden, and freshly baked sourdough, with the underscored caption, *'A healthy start to my day'*.

The room was thankfully warm, courtesy of the old-fashioned wood stove on which Dodge had cooked their meal. Yesterday, a massive electrical storm hit the area around mid-morning and raged unabated all day and night. The power had gone out around 8pm and had yet to be restored. Outside, the sky remained heavily cloaked with thick grey clouds, and a bitter wind could be heard whistling around the side of the building. Every so often, spits of rain splattered against the glass and ran down the window. The pale yellow light glowing from several oil lanterns flickered now and then when a particularly heavy wind gust rattled the panes.

Glad she had thought to pack winter clothes (her forward planning had never been one of her strong points), Pixie beamed at her companions gathered around the kitchen table. When she'd entered half an hour ago, she was relieved to see that Chad had yet to leave his room. Since his unexpected arrival a week ago, when she and Jordan had been fiddling with his truck, she'd been too busy to either think about him or seek him out.

And anyway, her daydreams were reserved solely for Jordan. Seeing him every Friday night, Saturday morning, and all day Sunday was sheer bliss. The way he'd stomp in, pretending he was being dragged along and yet his eyes always sort her out with an eagerness and heat that both humbled her and expanded her chest so tight she thought she would burst.

Yeah, life brimmed with more exciting possibilities than she'd ever dreamed about – and none of which now included Chad, the man she'd once believed was the love of her life.

Breakfast done, Pixie removed the plate and utensils she'd used to the sink, her thoughts winging straight to the guy who now occupied a vast amount of real estate inside her mind. Her head churned with questions. He hadn't turned up yesterday for the usual Sunday float-building event; instead, he had sent a brief text saying he had work to do on the farm. What kept nagging away at her was that although she had seen him twice since Chad arrived, his attitude, whilst still friendly, had been a hell of a lot cooler towards her - like he was distancing himself. There had been no questions about her ex, no admission of any curiosity whatsoever, which drove her crazy.

He'd given some flimsy excuse the moment the Friday night Japanese cooking lesson had concluded and fled, leaving her to sit alone in the library, missing his presence with an almost physical ache. And Saturday at his mom's gingerbread workshop, he'd been businesslike, his smiles brief, his expression inscrutable.

It was enough to make a girl scream.

Or think of something wicked – like how to torment him or how to drag him back into her orbit.

With a tiny sigh, she picked up her mobile again as she stood beside the table, her pulse zooming up a gear as she went to check her messages. It had been quite a jolt when she'd opened her emails yesterday morning to find a cold and rather blistering demand from one of the sponsors on her sites asking what the devil she was playing at. Lately, her posts had been diminishing in terms of both the length of content and the number of times she uploaded each day. The email had been a timely reminder that regardless of whether the urge to impress her ex remained her motivating factor, she had to keep in mind her influencer role was her job – like everyone else, she needed to eat. Who knew how many others would follow suit if this sponsor pulled the plug? As she logged onto her email account, she looked over at her extended family, her heart full.

Edwina, who had the most enormous multi-coloured hand-knitted scarf wrapped several times around her neck and which she had teemed with a fluffy pink pullover and zebra-striped jeggings that ended in a pair of line green gum boots, was busy heaping teaspoon after teaspoon of sugar into her cup of tea. Without saying a word, Tessa swiftly removed the cup, replaced it with a fresh cup of tea sans sugar, and tipped the offending beverage down the sink. Dodge was busy demolishing the last morsels off his plate with single-minded focus. After sneaking a peak at her parents, their youngest daughter, Tilly, slipped Boris, Edwina's dachshund, the last of her toast loaded with peanut butter, before jumping to her feet.

"Ready."

"Have a good day at school, sweetheart." Tessa held out her arms, and Tilly rushed over to have a cuddle before strangling her grandmother with a fierce hug.

"See you, Grannie. Bye Pixie. Come on, Dad!"

"Almost finished." Dodge gulped the remainder of his tea and pushed to his feet. Rounding the table, he kissed his wife on the cheek, then his grandmother, Edwina, before smiling at Pixie. "See everyone later on."

Snatching up a brown paper bag that held his lunch, he bundled Tilly into a parka, then shepherded her out the door, letting in a blast of cold air as he did so.

"That storm last night was extreme." Edwina looked thoughtfully out the window.

"Yes, Dodge got a call out for the SES around five this morning; he said something about a couple of fallen trees. No roofs or major flooding, thank goodness, although he texted later saying there was water over some roads in the low-lying areas."

"Sounds like they'll be busy the next few days getting our town looking in tip-top shape for the parade this week." Edwina turned to face her granddaughter-in-law.

"Tessa, we'll need to check on the chooks and get started on planting our winter vegetable seedlings. Do you have time today?"

Tessa nodded. "Already slotted in a few hours for doing just that this morning. I'll also clean up any fallen branches in our yard. What about you, Pixie? Feel like lending us a hand?"

But Pixie barely heard the question, all her focus was on her phone. She'd been waiting for her emails to load for the past five seconds with no results and now waved the offending piece of plastic in the air. Not even one bar lit up the screen.

"What's up with the internet?"

Tessa shrugged as she cleared the table and loaded dishes and cutlery into the dishwasher. "We've probably lost network coverage. It sometimes happens out here after bad weather."

"But...but when will it be fixed?" Pixie stuttered.

"No idea. It could be hours. Or could be days."

"Days!" Her voice rose to a shriek, remembering that almost offensive message she'd recently received. She placed trembling hands on the table, leaning over as if she needed something to steady her or she'd fall to the floor.

"I can't go days without loading content! I'll be ruined! My followers will desert me in droves! I have expectations to meet…"

Tessa rushed over to place an arm around Pixie's heaving shoulders as she swayed. "Hey! Take a breath."

Pixie gulped air, swallowing over the blockage in her throat. For a second there, she had almost succumbed to a full-blown panic attack.

"That's it. Nice, slow, deep breaths." Tessa's voice was soothing, steady, and so reassuring that Pixie could have burst into tears.

She gathered some semblance of composure, stepping back out of the other woman's embrace. What must they think of her losing her cool like a child?

"It's okay. I'm okay." She hesitated, then added, "Thank you. I don't know what came over me. No, that's wrong. I do. This is important to me. I want so much to succeed. I don't have a choice. Being an influencer is my only source of income."

Her chin trembled, and she sank into a nearby chair, meeting the women's concerned faces.

"I've tried so many different things in my life, and all of them have failed. Look at me. I'm thirty-six; I live rent-free in an ADU attached to my parents' house. If it wasn't for their generosity, I'd probably be homeless.

Now, finally, I'm making money, and I know I'm on a sure thing - that I will finally become successful and achieve a wonderful lifestyle."

"Sorry, but I must ask. What is an ADU?" asked Tessa.

"That stands for an Accessory Dwelling Unit, which is like a grannie flat." Talking had eased the tightness in Pixie's chest, and she slumped against the back of the chair, staring mournfully at her useless phone.

"I've got sponsors that expect me to post at least three times a day to maintain visibility – you know, so that their products I advertise on my sites receive maximum exposure. If I don't deliver, they will pull their sponsorships. Only yesterday, one of them threatened to do just that because lately, my posts have fallen off. What am I going to do? How can I find out when the network will come online again?"

Tessa began to speak, but Edwina drowned her out loudly and forcefully.

"The last time we lost coverage, it lasted almost two weeks." Edwina tapped the table with her finger. "But if I recall correctly, an area not too far from here still had mobile phone reception."

"Gran..." said Tessa.

Edwina shot her a fierce look, and Tessa closed her mouth and moved towards the sink. But Pixie didn't take a great deal of notice. She hung on to her first cousin's once-removed words as if the woman was an oracle from heaven above.

"*The Pot of Gold* farm," said Edwina.

Frowning a little, Pixie shook her head. "I've no idea what that is."

"It's a sheep farm, about forty klicks west of Bindarra Creek; it's just off Mt Ingalls Road and past Corella, but before you reach Boggabri."

The place names meant nothing to Pixie, but who cared? Forty kilometres. She did some maths in her head, turning it into miles. "I can do that. I'll use the car I hired from Billie. I'll be there and back again in no time."

"That's the spirit. But why don't you make the most of your trip? You could do some recording of the countryside on your way."

Pixie turned a doubtful glance at the rain slashing against the glass, but content was content, and she could make even a rainy day look interesting.

"True, and that will give me fresh vids for today. Can you give me proper directions?" Pixie was already on her feet, her mind leaping forward an hour or two to when she'd be able to post to her social media accounts.

"This is fabulous. Thank you, Edwina. You're a lifesaver."

Edwina lowered her head, saying softly, "Happy to help."

Tessa crossed her arms over her chest, her face tight. "More rain is forecast."

"Don't fuss, Tessa, and get me a pen and paper, and I'll draw a mud map. Now, Pixie, you take Mt Ingalls Road, then turn onto Rangari Road just past Corella;

you can't miss it. It's a dirt road. Then drive along for about thirty or thirty-five kilometres, then turn right onto a private road. There's a signpost there which says '*Nioka North*'. You just keep going until you see a sign to the *Pot of Gold* on your right. Just follow that road until you reach their homestead. Tell them I sent you, and they'll sort you out."

No sooner than Edwina handed her the mud map, Pixie was out the door and splashing through the puddles. She'd stashed her mobile phone, laptop, and a full water bottle inside her backpack and had clapped a woollen beanie over her hair. She settled behind the wheel of the ancient Toyota sedan, taking a long moment to orientate herself once more to the alien concept of the steering wheel being on the car's right-hand side.

Muttering, "Keep to the left. Keep to the left," she drove slowly out of the property, the windscreen wipers swishing lazily across the glass as a few drops began to fall, and onto Willow Tree Drive. She waved as she passed Mr Maki Fukuka who was walking a donkey of all things, along the road, a bright yellow umbrella held above his head.

Hands gripping the wheel as if superglued in place, she turned right onto Mt Ingall Road and, a few blocks later, had to slow down to a crawl when she spotted a warning sign about water on the road. She eased the car through, thankful that it wasn't particularly deep, then cautiously approached Gillies Bridge. She risked a quick glance out the window at the Akuna River raging with some force below, then accelerated past acreage lots that showed signs of the deluge they had experienced the previous night.

Water lay in puddles alongside the road, and in areas where the road dipped, it completely covered the surface. What with the way the road twisted and turned, not to mention how narrow it was in some sections, it wasn't long before a tension headache bloomed behind her eyes. The only saving grace was very little traffic on the road. All the same, she began to wonder whether she may have made a mistake. Maybe it would have been wiser to wait it out. Surely, it wouldn't take days for service to resume as normal. But she couldn't risk it; she had to post each and every day. That had been the terms of her agreements with her current sponsors. She had to keep delivering, or there would be no payday.

Jaw set, Pixie pressed her foot to the floor, only slowing when she spotted a sign announcing that a rest stop was ahead. It would be good to take a break, and soon, she was turning off the road onto a wide gravel area, where she stopped the car and got out to stretch her legs. A rumble of thunder growled in the distance, and she eyed the dark clouds, biting her lip as the intermittent raindrops increased in velocity.

About to climb back in the car, she paused as a small herd of six horses appeared through the trees. Throwing their heads high, they kicked out their legs as they charged around the paddock. Pixie ran for her phone and then began to record their antics, ignoring the rain wetting her beanie and clothes. Five minutes of awesome footage later, she stopped the recording and checked for a signal. Nothing. The horses trotted to a dense stand of trees, disappearing into the foliage just as the wind strengthened into a gale.

Shivering, Pixie became aware of her wet clothes and cold skin. And the fact that the rain shower had turned into a deluge. She scrambled to the car, fighting to shrug off her pullover from where it clung to her body as she settled behind the wheel. A few more tugs and she had the wet garment flung onto the floor, where puddles immediately began forming. She draped her sodden beanie over the dashboard. A quick check confirmed no one else was around, so she wrestled off her wet bra and pulled out an old tracksuit top she kept in her backpack for emergencies. She cranked up the heat once the car engine was switched on and hesitated. Pointless to turn back, given she had already driven so far.

With a nod, she put the car into drive and kept going until a few kilometres later, she turned off the main road onto what resembled a muddy, bumpy track. Barbed wire fences ran along both sides of the so-called road, and she had yet to spot a house or any sign anyone lived out there.

The rain was pelting down now, washing over the windscreen so fast it was as if she was driving through a river. The wipers squeaked and shuddered as they swept back and forth in a useless attempt to gain her some visibility. Hunched over the steering wheel, Pixie squinted at the glass, certain she had seen something. A dark shape. Something on the road. Something that shouldn't be there!

She slammed on the brakes.

The car jolted as one of its wheels landed in a pothole and spun to the right, its rear end skimming across the road as it fishtailed. Screaming, Pixie ground her foot as hard as she possibly could against the brake, her knuckles white-boned, where she held on for dear life to the steering wheel. The car came to a juddering halt, whipping her forward and back against the seat.

The drumming of the rain on the roof was deafening, obliterating the engine's hum and the swish of the wipers as she sat shaking, ears ringing.

Slowly, ever so slowly, Pixie relaxed her hold on the wheel and then closed her eyes.

A weight thumped onto the bonnet.

Heart threatening to burst from her chest, her breaths see sawing out of her gasping mouth; she peeked out of one eye.

A kangaroo was sitting on the car.

It leaned down to peer at her through the windscreen, where the wipers continued their fruitless fight against the onslaught of water.

Pixie frantically attempted to recall everything she had been told and knew about kangaroos. Okay. So they weren't carnivores. Meaning it wasn't interested in eating her. That was something. But they could be nasty, especially the bucks. What if...

Then...

What is wrong with me?

This is an amazing opportunity! Don't lose it, girlfriend!

Fingers trembling, she fumbled with the opening of her backpack which sat on the passenger seat, located her phone and began to record.

When the kangaroo lost interest in her, after all, she wasn't moving, just holding some oblong thing in front of her face; he stretched before taking a mighty bound off her car and into the bushes.

Pixie squealed. Stamped her feet against the floor and punched the air. Surefire winner!

All she needed was a signal.

She checked – still nothing. Not even one bar.

Sighing, she went to drive off.

The wheels spun.

But the car didn't move.

She pressed harder on the accelerator. The car's rear slid right, then left. The engine whined. Quickly, she eased off. Opening the door, she leaned down, blinking against the driving rain. The car was wheel-deep in mud and water and wasn't going anywhere soon.

There was nothing for it; she would have to walk the rest of the way. Since these farmers were Edwina's friends, they would surely help her escape her current predicament.

After securing her mobile inside her waterproof backpack, she stepped out of the car and popped up the umbrella Tessa had given her before she had left Fig Tree Lodge.

With the brolly tilted against the wind and sleeting rain, she began her trek down the road, keeping an eye out for anything that would point the way to the Pot of Gold farm. Just when she was thinking of turning back, she came across a break in the fence line and where a mailbox shaped like a sheep had been nailed to a post.

This had to be the place.

At least this track had been graded recently, although the heavy rain was beginning to gouge deep puddles that Pixie had to weave around to avoid. Ahead, the outline of a house took shape through the sheets of rain as she plodded on, teeth chattering, her body stiff with cold.

Off to one side of the house was a large shed where a truck of some description was discernible in the shadows.

A muffled bark sounded. She hesitated, but no dog came racing around the side of the house to savage her with sharp teeth.

What if no one was home? The thought took her breath away, but there was only one way to find out.

Feeling like she was a survivor of the Titanic, she waded to the porch, where she rapped on the front door. Thunder shook the earth. Lightning cracked across the sky. An eternity passed, a lock drew back on the door, and it swung open.

Pixie blinked.

No. It couldn't be.

"You!"

Chapter Eleven

For one crazy moment, Jordan wondered whether Pixie truly was standing in front of him or whether she was a figment of his fevered imagination. Then he rallied as a bitter wind swept a sheet of rain onto the veranda, peppering his face with icy pellets. No, she was real enough. His gaze travelled over her bedraggled form as puddles of water formed on the floorboards beneath her feet. Her face was pinched, her teeth chattered, and her lips blue from the cold as she shook out her umbrella, sending droplets in all directions.

"Bloody… Come inside, you're freezing."

"You're a lifesaver."

Visibly shaking, she dropped the brolly onto the porch, pulling off her soaked shoes and socks that landed with wet squelches. Then, slipping the straps of her back-pack off her shoulders, she shrugged out of her jacket and dumped it on the veranda as he stood to one side to allow her to pass.

"Ooooh, it's so warm in here." Lugging her back-pack, she stepped inside and gave him one of her amazing smiles.

"Fire's on."

Jordan shut the door on the bleak weather, then waved her through the archway to the left that fed into the main living room where the heavy curtains had been drawn across the two wide windows, and wood crackled and hissed in the open fireplace. All the lamps and over-head lights were on, giving the room a cosy glow.

CJ raised her greying muzzle from where she curled up in her dog bed close to the fire and managed a low growl. Followed by a yawn, then closed her eyes.

Jordan repressed a grin mixed with a bittersweet tug on his heart. Once upon a time, his dog wouldn't allow a stranger anywhere near the property, let alone inside the house. But she deserved her rest after over twelve years of giving her all chasing sheep and being the best dog friend a man could ever have.

His father, who was dozing in an armchair, rug over his knees, didn't notice the newcomer.

"Pixie, well, this is a surprise." His mother paused her knitting and gave the American woman a welcoming beam. "But you looked soaked to the skin, poor lamb."

"Yes, I'm sorry. I think I'm dripping onto your

carpet." Plucking at her damp jeans, Pixie looked down at her bare feet.

Jordan touched her hand, frowning at how chilly her skin felt under his fingertips.

"Good point. My sisters leave some gear here for when they come home, and I think Georgie is about your size. Follow me. A hot shower and dry clothes are what you need. Leave your wet stuff on the bathroom floor, and I'll pop them into the dryer afterwards."

He strode along the hallway and then indicated a room on his right.

"This is Georgie's room. The bathroom is next door."

About to head into the kitchen, he hesitated, placing a hand on the doorjamb. "I didn't see a car out front. How did you get here?"

"Oh, I drove. My rental car is stuck in the mud way back along a dirt track." Pixie rolled her eyes.

Straightening, he sighed as he spared a thought about how warm it was inside and how bloody awful it was out. Looked like he had no choice though.

"I'd better check it's not blocking the road. Either way, the car can't stay there. Keys?" He held out his hand.

Pixie dug into a side pocket of her backpack and held them out.

"How will you move it by yourself? I could help?"

"All good, I'll use the tractor. You need to warm up." Doing his best to dislodge thoughts of her soaping herself in his parents' bathroom, Jordan stalked through the kitchen, snatched up the tractor keys off a peg on the wall, then marched out onto the rear timber deck where he donned his old Driza bone coat, and placed an equally weathered Akubra on his head.

It wasn't long, and he bumped down his drive, then jostled over the cattle grid before turning towards the main road. His shoulders hunched as the wind howled and the rain stormed from the darkened sky with no sign it was letting up any time soon. Within minutes, the bottom half of his jeans clung wet and cold to his skin, but at least his top half was dry.

Pixie's car wasn't hard to find, and Jordan pulled up beside the stuck vehicle, tugging the brim of his hat lower to shield his vision from the storm. Leaving the tractor running, he walked around the rental and then crouched down to examine the depth of the mud coating the rear wheels. He emitted a groan. Damn thing was stuck all right. And unfortunately, the front of the car lay diagonally across the road. The storm had gouged a deep water-filled ditch on one side, while on the other, a tangle of blackberry bushes, scrub and tree stumps clung close to the road edge. Anyone coming to or from the main drag couldn't safely pass.

First, he positioned the tractor, then unwound the winch, hooking it onto the undercarriage of the small sedan. Next, he unlocked the car and placed the car into neutral. It was going to be tricky dragging the car out of the mud by himself, but doable; he'd performed the same action more than once during his lifetime. One of the many annoyances that was part of a farmer's lot.

An hour passed with Jordan firmly focusing all his attention on the task. He slowly and carefully dragged the vehicle free of mud and then manoeuvred it to one side of the road, leaving sufficient space for someone to pass. Feeling cold to the bone, he packed away the winch and tow rope and locked up the sedan before placing a few orange witch's cones he'd brought with him a couple of metres in front and then behind the car. Anyone driving along the road now had plenty of warning about a hazard ahead. Rubbing his chin, he climbed onto the tractor and drove back to the barn, his mind teeming with questions about his uninvited visitor.

The past week had been one of the worst weeks of his life. The image of Pixie strolling off arm in arm with the man she had professed to once been in love with had burned into his memory banks like sulphuric acid. It was an image that had tormented him with what ifs and maybe's and was the cause of the blue fugue he'd been wallowing in the past few days.

Seeing her at the cooking classes had been both bitter and sweet, especially as he didn't know how to broach the *'Chad'* subject and wasn't certain he was ready to hear what she had to say anyway. She certainly hadn't mentioned her ex, which led to both of them acting stilted towards each other as if they were strangers who had never met.

Strangers who had never shared confidences.

Strangers who kept slinging sidelong glances at each other and who tensed whenever the other was near.

And now here she was, and his curiosity about what on earth she was doing at his farm ate away at his sanity like a starving field mouse.

A few minutes later, the tractor was secured in the barn, and he was divesting his sodden clothes on the narrow porch to the small self-contained flat he'd built for himself. Coat he draped over a cane chair, hat he hung on a hook while he tipped his boots up so any water would drain freely from them. He decided to deal with his grimy socks later, feeling the urge for a hot cuppa and maybe even a buttered scone calling his name.

And, of course, the need to feast his eyes on the woman who had stolen every rational thought from his head since the day they had first met.

A quick hot shower warmed his blood and clad in fresh jeans with a waffle-weaved blue jumper, he pulled on a spare pair of gum boots, shrugged his old oilskin back on, and then crossed the short expanse of sloshy ground to the main house. After divesting himself of boots and coat, he strolled inside and into the living room, flexing his sore muscles as he went.

He found his mother showing Pixie a photograph album. They sat side by side on the couch, heads close together. His father was still asleep, the usually deep lines on his face unusually softened while CJ twitched and dreamed doggy dreams in her bed.

And for some odd reason, his chest tightened.

Pixie looked up the instant he entered the room, her gaze snagging his and holding it with such an intensity blazing in her eyes he couldn't look away if he tried.

"You were such a beautiful baby."

Oh my...! Kill me now!

"Mum!"

Hilary turned another page. "Keep your hair on, Jordan. I'm showing Pixie all my kids' photos, not just yours."

"Is this Jordan?" Pixie placed a scarlet-tipped finger beneath a large picture of a baby swaddled in a blue blanket with yellow ducks on it.

His mother drew in a slow breath. "No, that's Bart. Bartholomew, our first child. He passed away when he was only two weeks old."

Hilary stared down at the page.

Pixie touched his mother's wrist, saying softly, "I'm so very, very sorry."

"Thank you, dear. It was a long time ago."

Jordan moved over to adjust the rug covering his father's legs, giving his mother's shoulder a gentle squeeze as he passed.

"Were you able to move my car?"

Pixie snuck him a sideways glance, her tongue licking along the curve of her lower lip in a way that had all sorts of forbidden desires clamouring to be heard tumbling about in his brain.

"It's out of the mud, but I left it beside the track. When you leave, I'll drive you down to your car in the four-by-four; that way, I can be on standby – don't want you getting stuck again."

"I was just saying to Pixie before you came in that she should stay the night. I'll be too worried if she sets off for town in this weather," said Hilary.

The notion she'd be in his family's home - so close - and for an entire night dried every scrap of moisture from his mouth. But he'd understood instantly where his mother was coming from. Jordan nodded and then turned to Pixie, having to clear his throat so he didn't sound like a croaking frog.

"Don't mean to be rude, but why are you here?"

"There's no network coverage in town and I simply must upload content at least twice a day to stay visible and keep my sponsors happy. Edwina said yours would be working, so here I am. But your mom says yours is out, too."

"Ms Lette said that? Bit odd of her. Oh well," he mumbled, sucking in a steadying breath and thinking that statement over for a few beats of his frantic, aching heart. Okay, so she wasn't there to see or talk to him. Her visit had nothing to do with him personally. If only that realisation didn't hurt quite so much!

Suddenly, he was desperate to rid himself of her presence, take control, wrestle his life back to the way it was before she had strolled so casually into it and crumbled his illusions to dust. Not that he could blame her for something she was totally unaware of. In her eyes, but more to the point, a simple farmer like himself did not exist in the affluent world she inhabited.

He was invisible.

"I can take you into Boggabri in the ute. It's closer than Bindarra Creek, and you may be able to get a connection near the police station. Or we could try the RSL Club there. I reckon if we go now, we should be there and back again within two hours."

"No, Jordan. I don't want either of you on the road today. I've already told you she must stay the night. There's plenty of room." His mother's voice trembled and effectively shut down any further objection he intended to make.

His hands clenched, his pulse triggered into a gallop. They both knew first-hand about the dangers of driving a vehicle during a storm when the possibilities of flash flooding were as great as they were now. He cursed himself for reminding his mother of that terrible day when their lives had changed forever.

His voice softened as he accepted the inevitable and said, "Alright, we'll leave it for today - then, if we've still got no coverage in the morning, I'll run you into Boggabri, and after lunch, you can go back to Bindarra Creek."

He hesitated a beat, inwardly bracing himself for what no doubt would be a rejection. "Rain is supposed to be clearing tomorrow, and you could have a look around the farm if you don't want to head off too early. We could work on doing a promo video for the farm prize. I know we've already advertised it, but I was thinking a video might work better than those pictures I took with my phone."

Her steady gaze fixed on his. "We are so on the same page."

Face hot, he muttered, "In the meantime, I'll get on the CB and ask the coppers to swing by and let Ms Lette know not to expect you back today."

"Thank you." Pixie paused, taking the time to scrutinise his expression again before adding, "You're very kind."

"Always has been. Sometimes too kind." Hilary produced a tissue and blew her nose.

Eyes wide and sparkling, Pixie nestled closer to his mother. "Oh? What do you mean?"

"Maybe some other time," Jordan interposed, keen to switch the conversation topic away from himself.

"Hmm." Hilary closed the albums, resting them on a nearby coffee table, and rose. To Jordan, it appeared as if she was working hard to hide her smug expression.

"Hot cuppa time, I think. Then, I'll start sorting the vegetables for dinner. I hope you like a good old-fashioned roast dinner, Pixie."

"Sounds yum." Pixie pulled out her phone. "Do you mind if I do a quick video of your lovely living room?"

"Should be okay. Just don't take any of Tim, and please ensure none of the family photos are visible." Her smile as big as a house, Hilary left the room.

With a snort, his father woke and stared with some confusion at their visitor. "Who are you?"

"This is Pixie Wellington, Dad. She's Kirk's sister."

"Oh, right. The bloke marrying your girlfriend." He lifted a shaky hand, and Pixie immediately hopped to her feet to greet him.

"Never my girlfriend, Dad. Billie is a friend."

"Lovely to meet you, Mr Chase," Pixie said as they shook hands.

"Tim, please." His father glanced towards the window. "That rain I can still hear?"

"Yeah. It's teaming down. Pixie's staying the night. Mum's sorting us a hot cuppa, if you'd like a drink?"

Tim nodded. "Sounds just the ticket. I'm parched."

Leaning over slightly, he disengaged the locks and, using both hands, sent his wheelchair into motion. "Well, come on, you two. I wouldn't mind a gingerbread bikkie if there's any left. I heard you raiding the tin last night, Jordan!"

Pixie sent Jordan a puzzled glance, who quirked an eyebrow in response.

"Bikkies or biscuits are what you call cookies in the States."

"Got it," she said. "What's this about a midnight snack?"

Jordan snickered as he waved Pixie to follow his father along the hall. "I'm a working man. Gotta keep up my strength."

"Too many at your age, and you'll get fat. You're not getting any younger," said Tim with a snort.

Pixie giggled, then paused to lean down and give CJ a rub around her ears.

"Thanks, Dad," Jordan said wryly as they trooped into the kitchen.

"You play any games, young lady?" His father shot Pixie a glance beneath lowered brows as he positioned his chair at the end of the scarred timber table where they had enjoyed many a family meal together over the years.

Pixie chose a chair next to his old man. "Games? Do you mean sport?"

"Nah. Games. Chess. Monopoly."

Jordan and his mother exchanged a long-suffering stare and groaned. "Dad. She doesn't want to play a game of Monopoly."

He laid out a tray with china cups and saucers, the sugar bowl and the milk jug, carrying the lot over and depositing it on the table while Hilary poured hot water into the teapot. He brought over the biscuit tin, popping a few bikkies onto a serving plate. "Don't get conned, Pixie. Dad's a Monopoly fiend."

She giggled. "I'd love a game, Tim. I bet you one gingerbread cookie that I'll win."

His dad crowed with laughter. "You're on, young lady!"

"Seriously, you don't know what you've let yourself in for. Dad will play for hours."

Eyes twinkling, Pixie stretched out both arms and

linked her fingers together as she flexed her muscles like a fighter about to enter the ring. "I'm known in my family as the Monopoly Queen."

"Game on, then." Grinning, Jordan crossed to the old dresser and unearthed the box from a drawer.

They spent the next few hours engrossed in the game while the rain continued to thunder down outside, but it was warm in the kitchen thanks to the old combustion cooker Jordan had lit earlier in the day. In between their turns, Pixie helped his mother prepare the roast vegetables while he rubbed herbs over the leg of lamb under his mother's instructions. Once the meat was placed into the oven, he sharpened the carving knife with an old whetstone. It wasn't long, and the kitchen was redolent with the succulent scents of roasting meat and vegetables.

As they paused to replenish themselves with another pot of tea, Tim counted the piles of paper money in front of him as he said, "Won't be long, and you'll owe me that bikkie, young lady."

Pixie chuckled. "The day is not over yet."

"We'll see. You got a job? I don't want to see my son tangled up with another freeloader."

"Bloody hell, Dad!" Jordan set his cup down with a clatter and glared.

Tim Chase waved an airy hand, winking at Pixie. "Keep your knickers on, son."

She giggled. "Who was the freeloader?"

Her bright gaze swept around the table.

Jordan's mother was pursing her lips, an irritated frown on her face. "Really, Tim."

At the same time, Jordan burst out, "What Pixie does for a living is none of our business."

"I'm an influencer," announced Pixie, calmly rolling the dice and moving her piece four spaces ahead.

"You've lost me."

"Oh, Tim! Remember I told you about the American girl with an online business? Well, this is she," said Hilary before nodding at Pixie. "You just landed on my hotel and owe me a hundred dollars."

"Ouch." Smiling, Pixie handed over the money.

"Don't have a clue what you were talking about, woman," grouched Tim.

"Dad, I showed you her sites the other night!"

"Oh, that's you, is it?" Tim winked at Pixie over the exasperated heads of his son and wife. "Seems an odd kind of job."

Pixie shrugged. "I agree, it's not the same as a nine-to-five job in an office or being a schoolteacher, but I enjoy it, and so far, I'm making enough money to be independent. Just." She pulled a droll face.

"Didn't try anything else?" Tim asked, moving his piece several spaces and then chortling as he passed 'Go' and received more money to add to his pile.

Hesitating, Pixie mashed the remains of the biscuit on her plate into crumbs. She looked around the table, giving what almost appeared to be a cautious glance at everyone as if she was wary of how they would react.

"I've tried lots of things since leaving school. Nothing really jelled with me. If this doesn't work, I'm not sure what to do next."

Jordan reached across the table, laying a hand over her restless fingers. "You have a real eye for colour and style, and your content is both easy to read and interesting. I know you'll exceed your expectations."

His voice rang with the sincerity of his emotions, and for once, he couldn't care less what his parents read into his actions or words. All he knew was that he had to impress upon her how much he believed in her.

"Thank you." The way her eyes glistened as she gazed at him was a gift he hugged deep in the hidden recesses of his heart.

"Enough flirting, you two. I've got a game to win."
Smiling, Pixie winked.

And suddenly, Jordan remembered how she had winked at him before walking off with her ex. Cold to his core, Jordan returned his attention to the board.

Chapter Twelve

Pixie had risen before the birds the following morning; at least, that's what she assumed. Considering the day was dim and gloomy and the world outside shrouded in a heavy fog with little birdsong, the birds were probably hunkered down in their nests, attempting to keep warm. True to his word, Jordan had dried her wet clothes and left them, neatly folded, outside the bedroom door. Although Pixie was grateful for the loan of his sister's pyjamas, it felt good to be clad in her own long-sleeved t-shirt, pullover and jeans.

Shivering and rubbing her arms, she had made her way to the kitchen to enjoy a hearty breakfast cooked by his mother. After feeding his dog and checking on his father, who was still in his room, Jordan had invited her to don a pair of gumboots and a chunky overcoat, which, although was nothing to look at fashion wise, protected her body from the chill. As he pointed out various animals and enclosures, her eyes strayed towards the smaller dwelling which she'd been told was where he lived. Separate from his parents - and so very private. A thought that had her sighing inwardly at how she'd been firmly situated in his sister's bedroom. So far and yet so close to him, which had led to a night filled with delicious fantasies of sharing those private quarters with him.

His voice roused her from her daydream and into the present, a present that she had every intention of enjoying to the utmost. To her delight, she soon found herself feeding chickens, or chooks as Jordan called them, collecting eggs, raking out muck from their run and then out of the pigpen, along with feeding the pigs and a pair of button-eyed goats that had their own shelter and small yard not far from the house. Next, she'd been introduced to a couple of horses that had spent the wintry night snug inside the barn and shown the enormous vegetable garden and small fruit orchard. She could see that running a farm would suck up many hours of the day, but she also realised how committed Jordan was to his chosen lifestyle.

Food for thought.

But not now when she sat behind Jordan on an ATV, her arms wrapped around his waist, enjoying the warmth of his body so close her hers. Leaning closer, she yelled near his ear, "What's wrong with your father?"

"Accident which broke his back." Jordan blew out a loud breath, slowing the vehicle as they approached yet another gate that appeared out of the mist like a ghostly apparition. With a throaty growl, the engine died, and they both sat unmoving.

The silence of the morning was like a living thing surrounding them.

"Happened about twenty years ago now. A severe storm hit the region, and Dad was repairing a fence on the outermost perimeter of our property. Usually, we work together, but on this particular day, the SES sent out an urgent call for help when the creek and river both rose, threatening the entire township of Bindarra Creek. I was away from the farm for hours. Didn't get home until late that night to find the house dark and both my parents missing. When Dad failed to return, Mum had tried to raise me on the CB; as usual, our network coverage had failed, but I wasn't in my truck, so she went out looking for him herself."

"That's really brave of her; I don't know if I could have done that."

The gravity of the situation wasn't lost on her, and then she thought – twenty years. Jordan would have been, what? Twenty? Twenty-one? Not that old and already he had been active with the local emergency services and was running a farm.

Something that felt a lot like pride mixed with awe swelled beneath her breasts as he continued with his story.

"Most of the low-lying areas of our farm were flooded, so using another ATV was out of the question. After contacting the SES with our CB, I saddled Barnaby and went looking for them. Found them in the furthest paddock from our house. The land is very low-lying in that area, and a natural watercourse sometimes appears after heavy rain. Dad had been driving close to that course when a flash flood came out of nowhere, throwing the ATV off balance. The thing rolled, trapping Dad beneath, but luckily, it had been pushed by the force of the water towards the slope of a slight rise, and his head and shoulders were above the water line. When Mum found him, she somehow managed to shift the vehicle off him but was afraid to leave him; it was freezing that day, and he was soaked through. To give them a measure of protection from the wind and rain, Mum used her hands and dug channels, diverting the flow of water away from him. Then she made a rough covering using fallen branches and laid down beside him to keep him warm. Dad was unconscious when I finally came across them."

"What a terrible thing to happen to your poor Dad. And your mom – wow, what she did was amazing."

He said gruffly, "Could have been worse. He could have died out there."

"I suppose that's when you took over his responsibilities. Is that why you've never left the farm?"

"No. I love the life. Love being a farmer, love being a part of the cycle of life."

"But doesn't that mean you're the one ending lives? Sheep I'm talking about – not people."

She snuggled closer to the length of his back, smiling softly when his breathing hitched.

He twisted around, casting her a considering glance that sent the blood rushing to her cheeks.

"We don't raise our sheep for meat. Only wool. Our animals die of old age here, although some fall prey to wild dogs. A few accidents where they become stuck in deep mud before I can get to them or entangled in wire and are too hurt to be treated."

"You're quite isolated here, aren't you? In terms of hospitals and needing help for emergencies. Just like when your father was hurt."

"Comes with the territory of being a farmer in Australia."

He shrugged, loosening her hold, and Pixie eased back a tad. She was quiet for a few moments, mulling over his words, which had led like a river to the biggest question of all. From somewhere close by, a frog croaked, and a gust of wind rattled the gatepost while the need-to-know screamed like a chorus of those crazy, noisy cockatoos in her mind. Finally, she surrendered.

"Would you ever consider living anywhere else?"

His hands gently unlocked her fingers, removing her arms from around him then he swung from the vehicle.

She wished he would turn so she could see his expression, but he moved towards the gate, undid the line of chain, and began to pull the barrier open.

Then he was striding back to her, no hint of a smile on his face.

"Does it matter?"

Did it matter? Yes, it did, and suddenly, her heart was wedged like an immovable object in her throat. If she stood, she'd fall so shaky were her knees, making her grateful for the solid feel of the ATV beneath her. When had this guy become so important to her? Because he had – but the gulf between them had never felt wider – or as close. It was as if he had burrowed under and through all her defences, rendering her helpless under the powerful attraction that simmered between them.

Greedily, her eyes sought his, the hunger for more than a casual friendship gnawing like a life thing in the core of her belly. When she'd first met him, she couldn't make up her mind whether he was the strong, silent type or a good-looking guy with no substance. But now she understood it would take a lifetime to unearth each facet of this guy's fascinating personality.

What would it take for him to see her?

To see her, the real woman she'd kept hidden for so long.

But why bother?

In a few weeks, she'd be back in the States.

She'd probably never see him again.

She shivered, her eyes stinging as the wind blasted her face with an icy gust.

Of course, it was the wind.

Not stupid, silly tears.

While she'd been sitting like a mute statue, Jordan had retrieved the key from the ATV and walked back towards the open gate.

"You coming?" he called over his shoulder.

With trembling fingers, she undid and then removed her helmet.

The sky and land beyond lay encased in gently sifting fog, the frosty grass glittering like crystal stars, a monochrome in soft light greys and cool whites. A chilly breeze parted the silvery mass into strands of wispy fingers, revealing a group of woolly sheep with muddy legs staring at them with mild eyes, one of them baaing a greeting. Several of them appeared to be fatter than the others, and with a sense of wonder, she wondered if they were carrying their next generation. A pale caramel-coloured llama appeared like a magician, huffing out a warm breath that left white smoke like the contrails of a jet plane. His cute, banana-shaped ears twitched, bright eyes examining them as his trot became an amble. Then he stopped beside Jordan near the gate.

Jordan pulled off his helmet, tucked it under an arm, and grinned. He reached out and scratched the animal behind his ears.

"This is Pedro. He's a great guard dog. The best, aren't you, boy?"

"He's beautiful," said Pixie, meaning every word. Pushing aside her dismal musings, she hopped off the four-wheeled bike and placed her helmet on the seat.

Pedro wasn't disturbed by her approach, standing

quietly, puffing out his warm breath, as she petted his silky ears and soft muzzle.

"Guard dog?" she queried.

"Yeah, the llamas chase predators away from the sheep and alert us by giving a shrill neigh. I do the rest if I'm lucky enough to be close enough to hear."

"Wild dogs?"

To her delight, Pedro blinked his long lashes, giving her a soulful look when she stopped fondling him. She snickered softly, and ran a gentle hand down his long neck, marvelling over the silkiness of his thick coat. "What was that about wild dogs? You make it sound as if they're a problem."

"Defo, not only do they kill and maim our flock, but they prey on the native wildlife as well. Foxes are a big issue, too, and occasionally, we've had problems with dingoes, not to mention a few large feral cats. But I don't want to bore you."

"You're not. I find it all very interesting."

She snuck a peek at Jordan, a scorching quiver frizzled over her skin at the intensity of his stare. His eyes were so dark, like rich velvet chocolate, they were like his secret weapon. How come some lucky girl hadn't snapped him up? A memory popped into her head about his father mentioning *freeloaders*.

"I find that hard to believe. If that's the case, then why don't you have your phone in your hand? I thought you recorded every detail of every moment of your life." With that salvo, he swung away from her, indicating the open gate. "Come on. The grounds are too muddy from the rain, so we'll leave the ATV and go on foot. It's not far."

Clicking his tongue, Jordan strode off, the llama wandering beside him.

Pixie scrambled to follow, shivering as the damp and cold ate through her puffy jacket. From inside a pocket, she tugged out the knitted beanie Hilary had handed to her before they'd left the house and pulled it over her already mist-covered hair, ensuring her cold ears were fully covered. Already, her fingers were stiff, and she brought them up to her mouth to blow puffs of warm air onto them.

"I guess that was a fair point about my phone. But you know what, babe?"

He stopped and met her gaze with a steady one of his own.

"Lately, I haven't been that motivated to film as much."

"You've been busy, what with yoga, cooking and helping your family."

"Ooooh, sounds like someone's been asking what I've been up to."

His face flushed, and he ducked his head. "You're new to town, so everyone's keen to gossip about you. Look, I didn't mean to sound like I was judging. If I did, I apologise," he said gruffly.

"It's fine, but I appreciate your apology. Brrrr. It's so

cold. I always thought of Australia as hot." She giggled as she hugged her waist.

Jordan tilted his head to consider the grey sky while Pedro snorted before trotting off to graze over strands of grass that glittered as if they were made of ice.

"We get a bit of everything. According to the oldies, it even snowed near here one winter deep enough to build snowmen."

"Really? Wouldn't it be amazing, babe, if it snows this month before our Christmas in July festival ends?" She gave a little skip, lengthening her stride as a large building took shape in the silvery gloom.

"Yeah, that would be really something." He grinned at her and then nodded. "This is the shearing shed, obviously – duh - where we shear the sheep."

"You do that yourself?"

"Nah. We hire experts for that job. Got our hands on a great mob, banana benders they are, and they come down each year, staying in the bunkhouse for the duration."

"Banana benders?"

"Queenslanders. Maroon lovers." He winked as he unlocked the shed door and ushered her inside. "Queensland Rugby League football club's primary colour is maroon, which is also that state's colour. Ours is sky blue, just like our footy team."

Pixie smiled, shaking her head. "Like your football, do you?"

Hands on hips, she took in the strange-looking machinery, the various pens and the holding areas. Surprisingly, the air was clear with no hint of sheep dung, and her appreciation for Jordan's diligence grew.

"There is nothing like it; pity you won't be here for the finals. Now that's a fantastic day. Not to be missed. Probably score a tonne of likes for your vlog."

"I remember you told your father all about it last night. So, you really have seen it?" She inwardly rolled her eyes at how breathless she sounded. How eager.

"I've checked it out a few times. No biggie." He swept out a hand. "Want to see anything else?"

"I don't think so; it would have been great to see sheep shearing in action, though."

"Some other time," Jordan said easily as if some other time would actually happen. He led the way out of the shed, securing the door behind them. "Well, you've fed the chooks, thrown hay to the horses and goats and seen the shearing shed. Not a lot more I can show you in this fog."

"That's okay. I've enjoyed every minute of it. And to answer one of your previous questions, I did take some footage of the chickens and the goats; plus, I got a fabulous panoramic shot of the farmhouse with the fog shifting around it that looked a bit like dancing ghosts."

"Think you have enough good shots to make a decent video? Tessa tells me we've got heaps of entries for the major prize, mostly because the town is bursting at the seams with tourists. But I wondered if we could use a video to promote the region more. Would be awesome if we could pull in tourists for the rest of the year."

She touched his arm as they strolled towards where they had left the ATV. "Don't worry. Leave it with me. I'll make something stupendous."

"You'll blow them out of the water."

"You think so?"

He smiled, the brown of his eyes deepening to the colour of expresso coffee. "Hey! I've seen your work. And it's like I told Dad last night, I think you're amazing at what you do. I'm positive it won't take you long before you hit whatever it is you're aiming for. It isn't..." Jordan paused as he wrestled the gate back into place behind them. "I mean...I bet your ex is pretty impressed."

Now, what had he intended to say but decided against it?

He held out his hand for her to steady herself as she climbed onto the rear section of the ATV seat.

Oh, Jordan. You're such a lovely guy. I wish...

"He hasn't mentioned my job."

She left it like that, not sure if she was ready to admit to Jordan that the need to impress her ex had burnt down to little more than a spec of ash.

Jordan handed her a helmet and fastened his own before settling himself in front of her. He started the engine and raised his voice over the throaty hum. "He will. I'm sure you don't have anything to worry about in that regard."

And before she could ask what he meant, he set the vehicle into motion, and they were bumping their way over the rutted track leading back to the main house.

Chapter Thirteen

An hour later, they approached the small town of Boggabri, and Jordan slowed his ute as they passed the welcome sign.

Beside him, Pixie gazed out the passenger side window, her mobile held loose in one hand. She'd been quiet since they had left his home, and the itch to know what she was thinking was like a scab over a partially healed wound.

Clearing his throat, he muttered, "Boggabri."

Then cursed himself under his breath when she looked at him, a grin tugging at her soft lips. But she chose not to rib him over his inanely obvious remark, instead saying, "Where shall we try first?"

"I thought the RSL Club, as the Courthouse isn't open today."

"Good job." She turned her attention back to the window. "I appreciate you taking me here; I imagine you would normally be working on your property."

"That's true, but I had to come here either way. I have a doctor's script I need to get filled for Dad. Pain meds."

"I noticed he was still in his room when we left."

"Yeah, Mum said today isn't one of his good days."

"Should we do that first?"

"If you don't mind? That would be great as sometimes I have to leave the script if they're busy and come back later."

"Then, that's our plan." She nodded.

Approval and appreciation of his thoughtfulness for his father - hell, he wasn't sure exactly what was behind her brilliant smile.

All he knew, he felt all his Christmases had come at once. He turned off the main road and drove towards the town centre, where the huddle of houses around the main street was like children surrounding a campfire. Woodsmoke streamed from chimneys, and front yards were frosted white while the sky remained a sullen pale grey overhead.

It didn't take long to deposit the script, and like he had suspected, he was told to return in at least forty minutes.

Striding out of the chemist, he found Pixie had exited his ute and was filming the old-fashioned storefronts. Not that there were many. Boggabri was a small town, after all, and in decline, most people having moved away to the larger centre of Gunnedah.

"Okay, for us to walk to that club you mentioned? And could we go the long way around? I'd like to get a few more shots of the buildings here. I just love this architecture and look how wide the street is." She waved a hand about.

"Not a problem. We'll go to the end of the street, then turn around."

They fell into step together, strolling at a leisurely pace, and he was surprised that she didn't complain about their slow progress. He'd never been one for striding off as if he had a plane to catch. Something his mate, Billie, had loved to tease him about when they were kids. Not that he minded. Why rush when you'd get to wherever you were going eventually anyway? A few minutes longer wasn't the end of the world.

Apart from a handful of pensioners waiting inside the chemist, they were the only ones out and about, although, as they passed by, a cheerful conversation flowed through the open door of the newsagent where a burly farmer chatted to the person behind the counter.

"These buildings are so cute. How old is the town?"

"'Bout eighteen fifties, maybe? I believe the original township was a bit south of here and was destroyed by a flood before being relocated to its present location. If it wasn't so cold, I could show you Dripping Rock. It's a natural attraction where water seeps through the rock and flows fifty metres down into a rock pool. Great for swimming in summer."

"I'd love to see that; what else is around here?"

"Well, there's Gin's Leap, where legend has it a First Nation couple leapt to their deaths after they were forbidden to marry."

"Oh no. That's too sad." She shook her head.

"Almost forgot. There's Thunderbolt's Cave too. He was a bushranger back in the day and used to hide out in the hills."

"Now that I'd love to see! Sounds fascinating. I know very little about the history of your country. A bushranger, you say? Is that like an outlaw?"

He chuckled. "Your Wild West? Kinda."

"It would be fun to check out that cave."

A reel of glorious fantasies erupted inside his mind, where he and Pixie explored the local caves, swam in that rock pool and climbed to the top of Gin's Leap. She'd be a good companion; her natural disposition seemed sunny and energetic, and she gave the impression that she was perfectly happy by his side.

He cleared his clogged throat. "The post office may be worth a look. It's not far from the RSL Club. If you're not in a hurry, we could have a bite to eat at the club?"

As if in answer, her tummy gurgled. Pixie laughed. "I guess that's a yes for me. Let's bounce."

He grinned back at her, his chest swelling as she snuggled close to his side and linked her hand with his. "I'm famished, too. And there's another pub nearby."

"What – another one?" She gave a mock eye roll.

"What can I say? We like our beer."

Completely in tune, they continued their leisurely walk as they turned onto Brent Street. Ahead on the corner of Merton Street, a grey granite monument surmounted by an orb was stationed inside a small, partially fenced-off square.

"What's that?" Pixie held up her phone and took a few shots.

"War memorial to honour the soldiers from the town who served in the two world wars."

"You would have thought we'd have learned by now that there has to be another answer instead of killing each other," she said soberly.

Nodding, Jordan shoved his cold hands into his jeans pockets while she took more photos of the cenotaph.

When she finished, she placed her mobile in her back-pack, slinging it over her shoulders. Jordan reached for her hands, frowning a little at the coldness of her skin.

"Here, take my gloves. They'll be too big for you but will keep you warm." Pulling them out of his jacket pocket, he offered them to her.

"Thanks." Shivering a little, she slipped them over her hands. He had to repress his desire to pump the air when almost without thought – at least, that was how it appeared to him – her hand instantly sought his.

"I wonder how many more years will pass when memorials like this will mean nothing at all – except maybe to those who still serve."

She sighed. "Yes, I can see how the horror will continue to fade until people think of it as if remembering a movie they once saw - if they will think of it at all."

They continued down the quiet street until they reached the RSL Club. A few cars and mud-covered utes were parked out the front, indicating the club was open for business. After signing them both in, Jordan led the way through the building to the restaurant area only to fetch up short at the closed notice.

"Damn. I forgot the opening hours."

"That's okay. I was hoping for a burger anyway. Let's use the Wi-Fi, and then maybe we could find a café in town?"

"We walked right past it. The Bluebird Café is next to the chemist."

"Perfect. You can pick up your father's medication, and we can eat."

"Fancy a drink while you work?" he said as they made their way to a table in the main bar area.

"Something hot would be good if that's possible."

"I'll see what they've got." He left her to wrestle her laptop from her backpack and headed to the bar. He returned to their table with a couple of iced waters. "Sorry, the bistro isn't open yet."

Pixie paused, tapping on her keyboard. "Water is fine. Thank you. This shouldn't take long. I'm logged into the club's Wi-Fi and have everything ready to go."

Fifteen minutes later, they were at the Bluebird Café and had placed their order.

"This is more like it," said Pixie, placing her borrowed gloves on the table. "Lovely and warm. These heaters are doing a good job creating some decent heat."

They were seated outside the café where a half wall separated them from the footpath. The area was inviting, with several gas patio heaters blazing away and an insulated roof providing a buffer from the wintry chill. Not to mention the tantalising scent of frying bacon coming from the kitchen.

Jordan's stomach growled, and Pixie sniggered as she shrugged off her thick jacket. He'd already cast his off the moment they were out of the cold air, hanging it over the back of his chair.

The waitress appeared, placing a steaming plate of hot chips on the table, saying as she turned around, "Burgers are on the way."

"Thanks," said Jordan, already shaking salt liberally over the plate.

Grinning, Pixie leaned forward to snatch a hot chip. "There was something your father said yesterday that I wanted to ask you about - those freeloaders! Who were they?"

"Sorry about that; Dad was seriously out of line saying that you're one." Frowning a little, he pushed the plate closer to her, snatching up several chips and popping them into his mouth.

"Hey, I get it, he's looking out for you the best he

can. I like him, but he is a killing machine at Monopoly." She munched her hot chip, clearly enjoying the salty taste of hot potato as she ran her tongue over her lower lip as if to soak up every minutia of salt. She took another handful, sighing.

"These chips are to die for. I should have asked for my own plate."

"They are good. Just as well, I ordered a large serving." Jordan smirked. "Yeah, Dad loves that game. In case you're wondering, my parents and I don't think of you as a freeloader. From what you've told me, you work hard at earning a living, even if your chosen profession is lightyears from what we're familiar with."

"I understand it's not a career most people know a lot about. Take my family, for instance; they think I'm wasting my time. Like I always do."

Jaw jutting, Jordan covered her hand with his and gripped it tight. He hadn't liked the faint note of hurt he'd picked up in her tone. "I don't think so; it's inspiring how you've followed your dreams and packed so much into your life."

"You really think that?" Tilting her head to the side, she stared into the middle distance.

"Although..." He hesitated a few beats, then decided to hang it, get it out there, and be done with it. Honesty was always the best policy.

"I did wonder whether how much of what you do is participating in life or only observing it? Just a thought."

Eyes wide, she drew back in her seat. "Exactly what are you saying?"

He raised his hands. "Hey, it was a simple observation. No judgement here since I'm not one to talk. I spend most of my time either working on my farm or writing my next novel. That equates to a lot of alone time, hardly the mark of someone who is living life to the full. It seems to me, from what you've told me, that my way of living is very similar to your own."

"I never thought of it like that," she said, a tiny pucker appearing between her brows. "It's true that for a long time, I've rushed from one job to the next, never really stopping to think about where that was taking me. Making a success of myself – somehow – anyhow – has been my catchphrase for ages. I guess that partly comes from my upbringing. My father has spent my entire life trying to make it as a big movie producer while mom was always busy hunting for the next real estate deal."

He noticed that she hadn't mentioned how her ex had dumped her for a girl with money. "Families, huh. You know what they say, can't live with them, can't live without them."

"We love each other, I guess, but we live very different lives. My family are certainly nothing like what I've seen of your parents. You seem close."

"I guess we are, although looking back, we weren't always. I remember a lot of days coming home from school to an empty house. Running a property can sometimes be a full twenty-four-seven job – especially in times of drought."

"Or rain?"

"That too."

"You may be alone a lot, babe, but I don't think you're lonely. You're very involved in the community – what is it called now, the SES?"

He smiled, eager to deflect her probing questions even though he had started the discussion. "That's true. Well, we do have science fiction in common."

She grinned back at him, snatching more chips as the waitress brought their orders to the table. "Which still blows my mind that you are *the* C J Thorpe!"

"Who knows what other secrets I have hidden." He winked, then gave a gleeful moan as he eyed the loaded *'burger with everything'* on his plate. "Now, this is food."

They tucked into their early lunch with gusto.

"Those freeloaders?" She tapped him with her fork as she polished off the last mouthful of burger.

"Damn. Thought you'd forgotten about them. Okay, there may have been one or two girlfriends I invited to the farm for a lengthy stay. They weren't impressed with the life I'd chosen. In the end, it came down to moving to the city or the coast to be with them or staying in my hometown. You can guess what I chose."

Pixie wiped her mouth with a napkin, her gaze steady as if dissecting his soul with the precision of a surgeon. "Why? What's so special about a small town?"

He shrugged. "I like knowing I can stroll down the

street and at any given time, I'll see someone I know; people who I've known all my life, people that my parents and grandparents knew. It's a kind of connection I've never been able to feel anywhere else."

Pixie ducked her head. Drawing out her phone, she fiddled with the device, sending it spinning round and round on the table.

"The float parade is this Saturday. We've still got the finishing touches to do," she said, completely changing the subject, much to his surprise.

"We'll be fine. Both Dodge and I will be at the garage all day Friday, ensuring the truck is ready to roll."

"Will you be at Maki's last cooking lesson?"

He rubbed his chin and thought for a few seconds. "Much as I'll miss seeing you, I'll pass. I have chores to do when I get back since I'll be away all day Saturday."

"You'll miss me?"

"Figure of speech." Flustered and uneasy, he rose to his feet. "Okay, if we head back now? I need to check the livestock after all that rain."

"Sure. Sorry if I've held you up." Her voice was cool and stiff. "I've got work to do, too."

Sneaking a quick glance, he noted she was fluffing her hair and positioning her mobile in front of her face.

Again.

Or was she checking for messages? He berated himself for forgetting one very important factor. Chad.

Frustrated and more disappointed than he cared to

acknowledge, Jordan all but ground out, "Let's go then. We don't want to worry your boyfriend too much."

Lowering her phone a tad, she regarded him with an inscrutable expression for a few seconds, then said airily, "You're right, of course; we mustn't keep him waiting any longer than necessary."

With a toss of her head, she stalked out of the café and towards his ute, leaving Jordan feeling as if his heart had been torn from his chest and shredded into a gazillion pieces.

Chapter Fourteen

The dawn on Thursday morning of the float parade revealed a landscape shrouded in fog and frost. When Pixie leapt out of bed, she first hurried to the window to survey the weather, and the sight of all that crystal mist made her worry that rain would ruin the Christmas float parade. But that hadn't stopped her or her family from rushing to Fred's Garage after a hasty breakfast to give one last-minute tweak to the Lette family float. As the hour neared for the procession to begin, the fog bled away, leaving a cloudy sky and a very cold day.

And more to the point, no sign of any rain.

Stepping back from the float to obtain a better angle for her recording, Pixie gave a pleased hum, feeling the swish of satin against her legs and hearing the rustle of petticoats as she moved. She lowered her phone, muttering a soft *'woohoo!'* when she noticed the bars pop up in the right-hand corner. Finally, network coverage had been reinstated. Maybe she'd get time to upload content after the parade – nope, that wouldn't work since she had plans to experience the many stalls and the scheduled entertainment once the parade finished at the showground.

And those plans included having Jordan by her side.

Smiling a little, she brushed her hand against the long skirt of the old-fashioned, burgundy-coloured dress she wore, enjoying the feel of the satin against her skin. Her dress was complete with a real bustle, and she wore a lacey mob cap covering her hair. The entire family had dressed for the occasion in period costumes, and her heart skipped a beat as she peered around at the others, hoping – no aching – to catch a glimpse of Jordan.

After arriving back from those two amazing days spent in Jordan's company, she'd wandered around the Lodge in a bit of a daze. Her mind continued to replay their conversation. With a sense of wonder and immense satisfaction, she'd acknowledged that she'd never opened up to a man like that before, and never had a man been so honest with her!

However, there was one subject on which neither of them had touched; instead, they had skipped around it, even hinting at it but it remained unresolved.

Because there was no denying their worlds were close to being polar opposites. And where did that leave them?

Pixie was no fool. She knew when a man was interested in her, and boy, Jordan was very interested in her. But whether he'd act any further on his attraction was something she wasn't so certain of.

There was the tiny matter of Chad, too. But Pixie knew that was a moot point as far as she was concerned. Still, her ex turning up so unexpectedly had probably given Jordan a few anxious moments, and whilst she hated the idea he was suffering, she did nothing to alleviate them. Mainly because her thoughts were in turmoil. Her life had been that of a butterfly for so long, always running from one new experience to the next.

And she had enjoyed every minute of it.

At least, she thought she did – until a tiny town wound its comforting arms around her heart – and she met Jordan.

After a quick check of the time, she strolled up and down the line of floats, where some already had their engines running as they prepared to move out onto Main Street. Her followers were simply going to love this!

There was the fabulous late nineteenth-century police wagon drawn by two horses with a young farmer holding the reins. Grinning, he tipped his old-fashioned police helmet at her, then flicked a fly from his face with a wave of his hand. Abby and AJ were all dolled up in old-fashioned police uniforms, AJ twirling his baton for the benefit of a young woman in the crowd who was smiling at him broadly while Abby was petting the nose of her horse, Geronimo.

"This is going to be great," Abby said when she spotted Pixie.

"I'm so chuffed you went with my suggestion."

"Too good an idea to not use." Abby grinned and then indicated the back of the wagon with a tilt of her head. "And check it out – we've captured our first prisoner of the day."

Pixie giggled at Abby's husband, Roman, who was dressed in a white and black striped prisoner outfit, holding the bars and peering out mournfully. He winked and called out a friendly greeting.

"That is so perfect. I'll catch you later." Pixie switched on the audio and began to speak about the floats in detail as she moved further down the line.

Her favourite of all had to be the gingerbread house that Vito and Mandy had constructed to sit over his ute. Vito was tugging at his gingerbread man outfit while Mandy, dressed as Mrs Gingerbread, was checking over their supply of the cookies Hilary had baked and donated, which they intended to toss to the crowd.

Pixie just knew this float would be a sure winner with everyone.

But then again, she also admired the Emergency Services float. She kept filming as she strolled around the old red truck, grinning at the sight of the Santa mannequin dangling off an abseiling rig that was fixed behind the cab and ensuring she included footage of the realistic plywood cut-outs of Australian animals. Who didn't love a kangaroo? Or a koala?

"Ready to roll?"

And there he was, the guy who occupied her thoughts during the day and teased her dreams through the night.

"Wow, you look mighty fine!" Grinning, she surveyed him from the battered hat (he later told her it was called a cabbage tree hat – imagine!) that covered his fair hair to his knee-high Wellington boots, ensuring she filmed every inch of his costume.

Huffing out an exasperated breath, he rolled his eyes, but there was a hint of a smirk on his gorgeous lips that told a different story. He sure was getting used to Pixie recording almost every minute of her life.

That had to be a good sign – didn't it?

He'd dressed in character as a bushranger, with a waist-length jacket over a Crimean shirt, a thin strip of material tied around his neck, and moleskin trousers held up by suspenders. He'd even gone with a toy replica pistol thrust into the waistband of his pants.

He grinned and cocked his fingers as if they were a gun pointing at her. "Stand and deliver."

"Got it! Oooh, babe, that was fabulous," she squealed, then pressed the stop button.

"Glad to help, ma'am."

He tipped the brim of his hat.

"Time, people!" shouted Dodge from further down the line as he assisted his grandmother onto the back of the truck. He was dressed as a farmer and even had a piece of straw sticking out of his mouth. Pixie grinned as she watched Edwina irritably attempting to slap his hands away from her.

She and Jordan hurried back to the Lette float just as the marching band, which would lead the procession, started a spirited rendition of Jingle Bell Rock.

The crowd loved it, erupting into a roar and rousing cheer.

"Allow me." Jordan held out his hand and taking it, Pixie couldn't help but feel all kinds of dainty and protected when he shifted his hold to lift her onto the float.

Her brother sent her a wink, and she just had to do a quick recording of him striking a pose in his dandy costume, complete with a tall black hat and a cravat bunched around his neck, before tucking her phone away.

"I think you all look amazing. Now, you girls, behave!" Tessa called out as she waved to Kaylee and Tilly, who were dressed as late nineteenth-century schoolgirls and who both held onto the leads of a pair of sheep. Edwina sat before an old spinning wheel, looking rather splendid in a mob cap, pinny and servant's gingham dress. They'd gone with replicating an early Australian farm or as much as was possible on the back of a truck, and Pixie was impressed with the result.

"Don't forget Tessa, I need a film of every float in the parade. Oh, and the crowd, I need crowd shots too!" called Pixie.

Tessa raised her phone in the air. "I'm all over it!"

The driver's door creaked shut, and the engine started. There was a slight jolt, and then they moved onto Main Street, taking their designated place in the parade. Even down the slower end of town, a sizeable crowd lined both sides of the roads. Not just the townsfolk but a tonne of tourists that had flooded into the town a week before the designated school holidays had begun. Even Fig Tree Lodge had been booked to the max! But no one was complaining, especially the tourists who had embraced every event they could and eagerly spread the word via social media. Pixie had no doubt that should the town decide the festival would be an annual event, the crowds would only swell as time went by.

People whistled and clapped as the floats trundled past. Streamers were thrown from the crowd while Dodge, Pixie and Kirk tossed out brown paper bags filled with boiled lollies and either a pair of fingerless woollen mittens or a bar of homemade lemon-scented soap. The family had sure been busy since the announcement of a Christmas in July festival.

The parade moved slowly through the town where many businesses had gotten into the Christmas spirit, decking out their shop fronts with tinsel, Christmas decorations and multi-coloured lights. Pixie had already done several posts showcasing the varied ways different businesses and houses had dressed up for the festival. Her family had strung Christmas lights around the veranda of Fig Tree Lodge and the massive tree that stood pride of place in the front yard. Only three days ago, she'd gotten a fabulous shot of the vicarage, which had a lawn display of a Santa cut out and a painted wooden sleigh which was drawn by two white kangaroos (boomers Billie had told her they were called!) and which had proven a big hit with her followers.

Just before they reached the Riverside pub, they turned right onto the lane behind some shops towards the showground, where the various trucks and a couple of steam-driven tractors parked. All in all, the journey from the start to the parking area took a good forty minutes.

Rivers of people flowed into the grounds, and the atmosphere hummed with their excited energy.

About to step down from the float, Pixie paused when Edwina touched her arm.

"Come and see me sometime today. I've set up my usual fortune-telling tent. You can't miss it – it's gold and purple and called *Your Life in the Stars*."

"Sure thing."

Then her smile turned wide as Jordan appeared at the side, holding up his arms.

Leaning down, she fell into them, feeling them close about her body with a strength and purpose that sent goosebumps along her flesh and who knows why, but her eyes pricked with tears.

"Thanks," she said when she landed on the ground.

His touch lingered a few seconds longer before he stepped away.

Jordan tipped the brim of his hat, then crooked out his elbow. "Shall we?"

"Love to."

Slipping her arm through his, they strolled off. They headed first to where the participants of the various cooking classes proudly displayed their wares for sale and then made a beeline for a coffee from one of the street food vendors.

It was there that Pixie spotted Edwina's fortune-telling tent.

She surged ahead, tugging Jordan along behind her. "Let's get our fortune told."

A peek inside revealed no other customers, so she pushed him into the tent with a giggle, closing the gauzy drape behind her.

"Sit down. I've been expecting you," crowed Edwina from where she sat cross-legged on a plump cushion.

A small boho table was in front of her, and on it reposed a crystal ball (of course!) and a deck of cards. There was also a donation box detailing the Royal Flying Doctor logo on its side, and Jordan stuffed a folded note into the opening. A flickering light came from a candle, which also emitted a strong scent of jasmine, and a lantern was hanging from the centre of the roof.

Two short timber chairs were positioned in front of the table. Swishing her bustle to the side, Pixie sat down in one, pleased when Jordan followed suit without grumbling.

From a box off that Pixie hadn't noticed before, Edwina drew out a square silver tin that glittered when it caught the beams of the overhead lantern. Glancing first at Pixie and then Jordan, she opened the lid and grasped the contents between her thumb and forefinger. With smugness playing around her mouth, she intoned, "In my younger days, I was an avid reader of anything mythology."

Pixie snickered. "That makes sense, seeing how you're into fortune-telling."

"My favourite legends were the stories of Ancient Greek gods and, in particular, Astraeus, the Titan god of stars and astrology. As well as being the father of the stars, he's also associated with the four winds. Did you know that over ninety per cent of the matter in our bodies comes from the stars?"

Hands clenched over whatever Edwina held, she hovered them in the air several centimetres above the table as her gaze zeroed in on Pixie's face with the force of a deadly laser beam. "Not a believer, then?"

"I'm not sure. A couple of times in my life, I've experienced a premonition, and it has come true. So, maybe?" Pixie shrugged, battling a weird urge to slink under her chair and hide.

"And you, Jordan?" Edwina switched her attention to the man beside her.

He crossed his arms over his impressive chest and lowered his brows. "When I was a kid, I used to believe you were a witch. Now, I know better."

Edwina threw back her head, her long grey hair rippling over her shoulders, and cackled.

There was no other word for it.

And despite Pixie's belief that she was a hard-headed businesswoman, a woman of the world who could handle anything life threw at her, she couldn't stop the icy prickle flashing over her skin that stiffened the fine hairs on her arms. It required all her control to stop herself from rubbing her hands up and down her sleeves.

Edwina flicked open her fingers with a dramatic flourish, scattering tiny silver and gold glitter over their heads and hair.

"I invoke your hidden dreams with a sprinkle of stardust and golden sunbeams. Let the power of the stars enter your hearts and reveal yourselves; embrace this cosmic energy and go forth into the golden dawn of a new day."

Jordan didn't move; it was as if he had turned into stone while Pixie shook her hair and then brushed at where the minuscule sparkles had become entangled in the lacey bodice of her period costume.

"I wish you hadn't done that," she grumbled.

"Hush!" Edwina held up a forefinger, the single command resonating low and deep, before laying out a few cards.

"A four-card spread, I think, will reveal all we need to know. Ahhh. First, we have the sun card, beautiful Helios, responsible for the dawn of each day when he rides his chariot across the sky. He represents happiness, confidence and success. And...the awakening of a higher consciousness. But the question you must ask yourselves is, what exactly is it that needs awakening?"

Her glinting glance darted between the two of them before she continued. "Next, the Lovers. That needs no explanation. Now – this is interesting. We have the Tower reversed – hmm, someone is resisting change or the inevitable. It can also be perceived as the toppling over of all that has gone before. Fascinating how it is paired with the Lovers – which is right side up, of course. But which lover does it refer to?"

Edwina sniggered.

Where a second or so ago, she'd been icy cold, now a hot flash sizzled through Pixie's veins. She didn't dare look at Jordan, but tension vibrated between them, plucking at her already shaky nerve endings.

Edwina stabbed the last card with her forefinger. It was a beautiful, primarily gold-coloured image of a star with eight flickers of flame and eight lances shooting from its orb in a yellow sky background, studded with five-pointed small glittering gold and silver stars.

"And here we have it – the Star card, a stellar deity. One of my favourites. It's a card of power that means anything is possible, and your dreams can come true. More than that, it is a card of hope, of aspiration, of elevating yourself to the very stars themselves. It's also the card of personal growth, but..."

Here, she paused and examined Pixie's face as if drilling through to her most secret yearnings.

"With the reversed Tower close by, your beliefs will need to be torn apart to reveal hidden dreams quite different from what you think you know, dreams which will come true – for both of you. But only if you heed the message in the cards." Her finger rested on the Lovers card, and she leaned forward, her eyes beady and bright as she stared at them.

Silence fell inside the small tent, making what had at first felt cosy and comfortable now stifling and confining. And Pixie couldn't handle being there any longer; she had to escape.

She sprang to her feet as if propelled by rocket boosters, muttered her thanks and plunged aside the gauzy curtain to emerge out into the cool, crisp afternoon.

Edwina's voice shouted from the tent, "Don't forget to check out Mary Mooney's Kissing Booth!"

"Well..." Pixie gulped air like she was an undersea deep-water diver coming up to the surface.

Beside her, Jordan pushed his hands deep into his jacket pockets. "She's your relative." He sounded relieved, as if that simple fact would somehow distance himself from the entire experience.

"You've known her longer." Pressing a hand to where her heart was finally beginning to slow its frantic pace, Pixie turned to him.

"Weird how she said that strange incantation about hidden dreams, the dawn of the day and then laid out the Sun card. I wonder what it all means."

He refused to look at her, keeping his gaze fixed on

something beyond her shoulder. "Ms Lette was probably talking about you and your ex getting back together. She's renown for meddling in people's lives. I bet she had those specific cards all ready for when we entered her tent."

"You think that's all I want out of life? Getting back with Chad?" Lifting a hand, she prodded his chest with a finger in tune with each word she all but shouted at him.

"Isn't he the one you've wanted to impress all these years? The reason why you've never been able to settle with anyone else?"

They stood glaring at each other for several seconds until Jordan broke off his gaze first to nod in the direction behind her.

"Speaking of he who shall not be named, here he comes." He scuffed his boot against the hard ground. "Look, I was out of line there."

"Is that an apology?"

"Sorry if I'm interrupting, but I need to speak to you, Pixie," came a gruff voice before he could respond.

And then Chad was standing next to them with her brother hovering a few feet away. Neither guy looked particularly happy; in fact, Chad was pale with a few beads of sweat lining his forehead despite the cold day.

"I can leave." Jordan made to move off.

But Chad threw out a hand. "No, unless that's what Pixie prefers."

Now, that was a turn-up for the books! Folding her arms around her waist and not wanting Jordan to disappear until they'd sorted out a few things, Pixie said, "It's fine. What's going on?"

"I'm leaving in a few minutes. I arranged for a private charter to take me to Sydney, where I'm booked on a flight back to the States."

Chad cast his eyes to the sky for a moment, then emitted a heavy sigh. When he looked back at her, it was as if he had aged ten years.

"I'm a coward. That's why I'm here. And probably why I took so long to tell you I wanted out of our relationship. You were right to hate me. Everything you told me about how mercenary I was – am – was true. Yes, I left you for Lisa because she could give me an amazing life that I would probably never attain for myself. At first – everything was wonderful. I thought money solved everything, but I finally realised that it doesn't. We've been trying for a baby for ten years and tried it all. Nothing worked. We were lucky three times with IVF, and three times around the six-week mark, Lisa miscarried. Our last hope was surrogacy, only for that to follow the same pattern. That occurred six days before I hopped on a plane and ran. No idea what I thought I was doing, all I knew was that I couldn't face Lisa, I couldn't help her. I couldn't give her what she wanted above all that money she inherited from her parents. I know it was a dreadful way to act, especially as Lisa needed me more than ever."

He stopped.

Pixie's heart welled with empathy for the woman

who had once been her best friend since middle school. And for the guy she had once loved. "Oh, Chad. I'm so sorry. Poor Lisa, what a heartbreaking ordeal for her – and you. But why come here?"

"Kirk's been my best buddy for like forever. I thought I could talk to him. Plus, it was the only place I could think of that was far enough away. But now that I'm here, and spent time in this place and had some space to think, I've finally realised why I felt so useless, such a failure. The thing is, Pixie. Somewhere during the past fifteen-odd years, I fell in love, and I've come to realise that all that wealth means nothing. It's Lisa and her happiness that consumes my every waking thought. She's my everything. But will she forgive me for leaving her?"

Jordan stirred. "All you can do is tell her everything you've just told us. And hope for the best."

"Jordan's right." Pixie threw him an admiring glance before turning back and taking Chad's hands in hers. "And then, once you've sorted yourselves out, come back to us. We'd love to have you here to celebrate your best buddy's marriage."

"We're all good then?" Chad said hoarsely.

"We're good." After giving his hands a squeeze, Pixie dropped them. "Now, don't you have a plane to catch?"

"Yeah. Yes, I do." A tremulous smile formed on Chad's face. He pulled Pixie towards him, gave her a hug and hurried off with her brother on his heels.

Pixie stared after them for a while before searching

Jordan's face. What did he feel after hearing Chad's confession?

How did she feel?

He beat her to it before she could decide exactly what she wanted to ask.

"I think you're amazing how you handled that situation."

She gave a self-deprecating shrug. "I really felt for them."

"Are you okay?"

"I rather think I've been okay for a while now. I just didn't realise it," Pixie said slowly.

A tiny frown appeared between Jordan's eyes, and he rubbed his chin.

The tense silence bristled between them.

Until...

"I need to think," they both blurted at the same time.

Without another word, Pixie rushed off. She spent the next couple of hours wandering amongst the street food stalls, searching her soul and heart until her steps led her back to Fig Tree Lodge.

Chapter Fifteen

His mind filled with purpose and his body brittle with edgy tension, Jordan scanned Lette Park but failed to spot the owner of his heart. It had been twelve days since he had seen her last. Twelve long, hard days during which he quickly came to accept she wasn't leaving his heart any time soon.

Nope, she had definitely taken up residence there, and it was time for him to do something to ensure it remained a permanent arrangement. By some weird unspoken agreement, neither had phoned nor made any attempt to broach the conversation about where their attraction was heading – if anywhere. Instead, Jordan had kept as busy as possible, working on the farm, plotting the outline for his next book, and making his section of their gingerbread house display. He knew from her brief text messages that Pixie had also been busy. If she wasn't texting him to nut out the more in-depth details of their gingerbread project, she was knee-deep in involvement with her brother's wedding.

Much to his mother's mock horror and his father's amusement, both he and Pixie had decided not to go with a traditional gingerbread house, but rather, they had dreamt up a science fiction scene. He'd been charged with making and decorating a replica of the Starship Enterprise and a Stargate ring. Pixie's tasks included making various sci-fi characters, a British telephone box, and, of course, a kangaroo, which she had insisted had to be included. Jordan had also made the base, which he'd fashioned out of MDF board, and painted it a lurid purple at Pixie's request. They had used a tonne of liquorice all sorts, chocolate buttons, lolly snakes and marzipan for the decorations.

They had both been happy with the final photos they had sent each other, and his mother had driven into town last Saturday for the final cooking class session with Jordan's section, Pixie having taken on the task of assembling it. He had had every intention of going himself until a mini emergency had erupted when he'd found one of his sheep injured, having been attacked by probably a wild dog during the night. That meant he had spent most of the day with the vets until the poor animal was out of danger.

He rubbed his chin and helped his father out of the car and into his wheelchair. While his mother fussed about tucking a rug around his father's legs, Jordan took another look around the park.

There was no need to panic. Pixie was probably here, somewhere; it was just that he couldn't spot her, which wasn't surprising given dusk had fallen and the park, although well-lit by lamp poles, was still full of shadows and hidden corners. Plus, even from where he'd parked the car, he could see quite a crowd had already arrived. People queued in front of the street stalls and hot food stands. Some were picnicking on rugs on the grass, while others sat at a few plastic tables and chairs that had been positioned near the food section. Kids ran everywhere, hyped up on food and anticipation of the night ahead.

A series of bangs and a shrill drilling noise came from the direction of the stage erected for the light show. Since the town had banned fireworks, tonight's event was going to be a drone light display organised by Troy Davidson and Toby Stinson. And since those two blokes were in charge, Jorden knew the event would be spectacular. They'd talked of nothing else whenever he caught up with them at the SES meetings.

What made this final event for the town's first Christmas in July festival so very special was that the weather had cleared. Although cold, with sufficient chill to numb the tip of his nose, the night was still with no wind, and the sky was bright with crystal-white twinkling stars.

Beautiful.

And perfect for his purpose.

"We're going to grab something to eat. I can smell those hotdogs and sausage rolls from here. You coming Jordan?" His mother began to push his father's wheelchair along the concrete footpath.

"Not just yet, thanks Mum. Thought I'd look around first."

"Hah!"

She wasn't fooled. The grin she sent him was knowing as she stopped, turning the chair so both his parents faced him. "I'm so happy for you, darling."

"Mum!" he groaned, hunching his shoulders as if he could disappear inside his fleecy jacket.

"I know I spoke out of turn. But your father and I just want to say that please, please, do not factor us into any decision you intend to make. Or have made already. We'll be fine. The farm will be fine. Won't it, Tim?"

"Yes, son. Your mother's right. We've been talking things over and decided we can hire a foreman to look after the farm. I can do all the admin stuff and project manage him. I think it'll be good for me to contribute again. I'm looking forward to it."

Taken aback, Jordan looked from one to the other. Since his father's accident, he had taken on running the farm solely by himself; at first knowing that his father had a long road in front of him health wise and wasn't able to help. But afterwards? Had he been too controlling? Assumed where he should have asked?

"Jordan, you've done a damn fine job, son, and I'm both proud and grateful for everything you've done. But we're saying that if your life needs to follow a different path, then we're all good. We'll manage." Tim reached out a hand, and when Jordan took it, his father gripped it with surprising strength.

His eyes burned behind his lids, and he had to choke down the constriction welling in his throat.

"Thanks, Dad. Mum. I appreciate that."

"Well, that's that. Now, Hilary, where's that sausage roll you were talking about?"

His mother came over and kissed his cheek. "Good luck, darling. Come and see us later, okay?"

"No worries."

After making a small shooing motion, Hilary wheeled his father down the path, and as they went, Jordan could hear them greeting friends and neighbours.

Taking a second to adjust his beanie lower over his cold ears, Jordan began his search. From the stage came the screech of the microphone as the mayor bellowed out a short welcome speech, then, without fussing around too much, drew the winner of the farm weekend. The name wasn't one Jordan recognised, which hopefully meant the prize had gone to a tourist. It was greeted with excited yells and cheering as a family of five rushed to the stage.

Another Christmas song crackled through the speakers, and the scent of sausages sizzling on a barbeque was ripe in the wintry air.

Threading his way through the crowd, he finally found Pixie chatting with her extended family, who were sprawled on the large picnic rug or sitting in a few camp chairs. She sat cross-kneed and held a thermos mug in her hands and looked so beautiful to him, that he stopped and stared, his throat constricting with sudden emotion. Steam curled from her mug as she took a sip. Then, as if she'd sensed his presence, she raised her head, her gaze seeking and immediately finding him.

A smile brighter than the sun spread across Pixie's face.

"Babe!" she shrieked, leaping to her feet and running towards him.

Whatever misgivings or doubts he had entertained vaporised as if they had never existed. He opened his arms wide, pulling her into his embrace, then locked her in tight. Hot liquid spilled over his hand, but he flicked it away, dimly hearing the soft thud as the thermos mug landed on the grass.

"You came," she whispered, her voice muffled from where she pressed her face into his chest.

"Always."

She pulled away, her fingers still curled in the front of his jacket like she was loathe to let go, her face alight with mischief and, dare he say...joy.

"Let's check out our gingerbread display. It is totally crushing!"

And thankfully, if they did so, they'd be well away from her family's inquisitive eyes.

"See you later," he muttered to them as he and Pixie hurried off.

"I've missed you," he said first.

She snuggled against him, their hands tangled together. "Totally same."

Their steps slowed, then spying a pathway that was relatively clear of other people; Jordan tugged her to the right, leading her away from the crowd.

"You first," she said, sounding breathless.

"No. This first." Cupping her face in his hands, he stared at her for a good sixty seconds, suddenly wordless and a little unsure.

But she imitated him, shifting closer.

"Yes, please."

Finally, their lips met, fusing together in a kiss that kept going and going. It was as if they had been apart for centuries and had now found each other again. It was as if they belonged.

Easing apart to breathe, Jordan found his voice.

"I've wanted to kiss you since the moment I first saw you."

"If you had, I would have biffed you on the nose. I was far too hung up on an agenda that no longer matters."

Jordan sighed, turning so their cheeks pressed together. "I love you."

"I know, babe. And I am completely into you." She sucked in an audible breath, and he felt her stiffen a little against him as if she might be a tad anxious about his reaction to what she intended to say next.

"I've come to realise I don't need the fame of a mega

social media star to be happy. A life rich in true friend-ships and living alongside the kind of man who will protect and value me for who I am is one that sparkles a lot brighter than anything I could ever imagine. I want to stay – here with you and live a small-town life – if you'll have me."

"Are you mad?" he said in a teasing tone. "Can't you feel how much I want you?"

She giggled and then uttered a contented sigh.

"Just as well, babe. Or I'd have to convince you."

Lifting his head, he nuzzled her hair, then brushed his mouth against her jawline.

"I could do with a little more convincing."

The next few minutes, they were busy, each doing their best at *'convincing'* until, with an engaging giggle, she pushed against his chest to stare into his face.

Her lips were rosy, her eyes sparkling, and he could have broken into song as sheer happiness swelled inside his chest.

"Well, aren't you going to ask me?"

He grinned.

"Pixie Wellington, will you marry me?"

"Yes!" She flung her arms around his neck and held on tight. For his part, he wrapped her close, feeling he never wanted to let her go.

"We have a lot to discuss," he muttered, inhaling her soft, apple-scented hair.

"We'll work it out."

"You sound confident."

She smirked. "It's all in the bag, babe."

"Dad intends to take on more of running the farm. We won't always be living a small-town life. I've got plans." He winked.

"No, I'm the one with the plans."

He gave a mock groan. "Somehow, I knew that's what you'd say."

Then he had to give her another kiss.

Which led to a whole lot more.

Epilogue

"I now pronounce you husband and wife. You may now seal your vows with a kiss." Pastor Miller's voice rang like a clear clarion call and echoed through the small church of Saint Ignatius. Like the promise of gold at the end of the rainbow, sunbeams streamed through the beautiful stained-glass windows, and the watching crowd of family and friends held their collective breaths.

From where she stood as best woman for the groom, Pixie peeked around her brother, catching Jordan's eyes, and they exchanged a smile. A smile that brimmed with anticipation, happiness and hope for their future together.

Not wanting to steal any of Kirk and Billie's thunder,

they kept the announcement of their pending nuptials to themselves. Not that that would remain a secret for very long, Bindarra Creek being what it was – a hotbed of rampant gossip. But in the majority, it was well-meant and rarely malicious. Rather than subject her parents and her other brother to another flight to and from the States, they had decided on a simple styled wedding to be held on the grounds of Fig Tree Lodge, the historic family home, and hoped to have it organised, done and dusted before Pixie's family were due to fly back to LA. That didn't leave them a lot of time – a mere two weeks, but Pixie was confident they could organise everything with time to spare.

As her brother swept his new bride into his arms, she gripped her posy tighter, the events of the past months flashing through her mind like a video. She had arrived in April, confident and sure in her goals in life, only to have what she'd believed to be her dreams torn apart and a longing she'd rarely acknowledged, awakened. A longing to be loved and respected by a special guy of her own.

Fast forward to early August and the here and now; who would have thought she'd find love in a small town on the opposite side of the world? Not to mention a future she had never imagined but one she intended to embrace with all her usual enthusiasm and energy.

She'd truly had hidden dreams - and she knew without any doubt whatsoever that Jordan had held the same.

Swinging a radiant Billie around to face the congregation, Kirk held a hand up in the air and shouted, "Yes!" much to everyone's amusement and appreciation. Clapping and cheers echoed around the space as they shared in the couple's happiness. Even Mr Miller lifted his head, his cloudy expression clearing with recognition for a few moments as his gaze rested on his daughter. Immediately, Billie went to his side and slipped an arm gently around his frail shoulders. Placing a kiss on his cheek, she took over, pushing his wheelchair down the aisle one-handed, the other resting on her six-month baby bump. That dress had had to be adjusted at least four times over the past six weeks, with Edwina declaring Billie must be having triplets since she was so big! Every time Edwina made those wild assertions, Billie and Kirk paled while Pixie giggled, hoping that yes! she'd be an auntie at least twice removed.

With Billie smiling at her friends and family, she moved towards the church door with her father. Behind her, her new husband, Kirk, walked arm in arm with Pastor Miller, Billie's mother. Pixie surged towards Jordan, and they held hands as they followed the two flower girls, Kaylee and Tilly Myers, with the other bridesmaids and groomsmen trailing down the aisle last. Billie had chosen soft rainbow colours for everyone's outfits, and even the guys were decked out in pastel-coloured suits – the entire effect was one of colour and joy. Pixie intended to go with an all-white colour scheme for both the bridal party and the guests, offset by brilliant sprays of purple and blue flowers.

But that was in the future.

Today belonged to her brother and her new sister-in-law.

About halfway down the aisle she spied Lisa sitting alone in the pews, looking far too thin and pale. Pixie gave her a little wave, and she felt grateful when the other woman nodded back, her eyes glassy with unshed tears. Once upon a time, they had been inseparable as friends; perhaps one day something of their former closeness could be salvaged. Pixie sure hoped so.

The bridal party stepped out of the church to begin the hour-long ordeal of having their photos taken before they could head to the Lodge for more photos and then the reception. As the others began to form a circle around the bride and groom, she just had to hug the man of her dreams, loving how his arm snaked around her waist, melding her body against his.

The crowd jostled forward, gleefully tossing rice and colourful streamers all over the place.

Pixie caught sight of Edwina Lette and Jordan's parents, looking far too pleased with themselves and not bothering to hide their broad smirks. They gazed at her and Jordan and then spoke to each other.

Leaning closer, Jordan nibbled her ear lobe before whispering, "I can't wait to tell them our news."

"Same, babe. Although I suspect they already know,

it will be wonderful to have our news out in the open," she breathed back, wondering when she could drag him to some hidden corner and kiss him. "Maybe tomorrow?"

"I like the way you think, sweetheart."

He drew back to search her eyes. "Any reservations?"

"No way! I've got our life all planned, babe. You, me, maybe some mini-you's, and mini-me's if we're blessed, lots of camping, shearing sheep, you writing, me vlogging, going to sci-fi conventions together!"

She gave a muted squeal, almost jumping out of her high heels at the very thought of the life ahead and wanting to do an impromptu dance movement on the church steps.

"And I've got plans for this town of ours thanks to my awesome social media skills. It's going to be great, babe, you wait and see."

~ The End ~

Thank you for buying *Hidden Dreams*. I hope you enjoyed Pixie and Jordan's love story and re-visiting our fictional small town. This was one of those books which just about wrote itself - I could see Pixie and Jordan so clearly in my mind. And, as always, I love writing in the Bindarra Creek world with its cast of fabulous characters.

Next up is my gingerbread recipe and more details about the Bindarra Creek Christmas in July Romance series. Please read on.

Gingerbread Biscuit recipe:
Ingredients:
1 ¾ cups wholemeal self raising flour

1 ¾ cups white self raising flour

½ teaspoon baking powder.

1 egg

1 large teaspoon vanilla essence

150gm butter

¾ cup maple syrup

½ or ¼ cup raw sugar

3 or 4 tablespoons ground ginger

2 tablespoons ground cloves

1 tablespoon ground nutmeg

2 tablespoons ground cinnamon

1 heaped tablespoon fresh crushed ginger (optional – as you can see I love my gingerbread very spicy!)

Method:
Beat softened butter and sugar together until creamy, add maple syrup and fresh ginger and beat until combined. Add vanilla essence and egg, beat until combined.

In separate bowl, add the dry ingredients and mix until combined. Mix all ingredients together gently with wooden spoon. Do not over knead or beat, and you will want the mixture to be moist, thick and sticky. Dust hands with extra flour and divide mixture until two and form into oblong shape. Wrap both in clingwrap and refrigerate overnight (or at least 3 hours).

NB: If you are not a fan of wholemeal flour, then you may need to reduce the maple syrup and sugar (I find white flour doesn't require as much syrup and sugar – however, I also do not like very sweet biscuits – you may need to tweak the ingredients to suit your own taste.)

Cooking:

Warm oven to about 180 degrees C (fan force), line tray with baking paper. Dust rolling pin and board with flour, roll out one of the dough mixtures and use biscuit cutters for shapes. Dough should be about 0.6cm thick. Bake for about 8 minutes if the biscuit is 10cm or smaller, and bake about 11 minutes if cookie is larger. Biscuits will be golden brown when ready and still soft to the touch if you press your fingertip lightly to the surface. Remove from oven and allow to cool. The result will be a gingerbread biscuit that is soft inside and slightly crisp on the outside. If you prefer a crunchier texture, bake for a few extra minutes.

Best served with a cup of freshly brewed Chai Tea!

Note from author: *This recipe has been adjusted to my personal taste from one of my fav on-line baking sites (Sally's Baking).*

About the Multi-Author Bindarra Creek Christmas in July Romance Series

Welcome to Bindarra Creek, a struggling country town where people work hard and love deeply. Set in the picturesque tablelands of New England, Australia, Bindarra Creek is a fictional, rural community full of romance, intrigue, adventure, drama and suspense.

This latest series, **Bindarra Creek Christmas in July romances,** is the seventh multi-author *'series'* set in the fictional small town of Bindarra Creek. The books can be read in any order and each book features a stand-alone romance.

Hidden Dreams – Suzanne Gilchrist
Cooking up Christmas – Susanne Bellamy
Hearts in Harmony – Annie Seaton
It Might be You – Juanita Kees
Second Chance Christmas – Kerrie Paterson
A Winter's Promise – Rhonda Forrest
About That Dance - Linda Charles

The other series are:
Bindarra Creek Small Town Christmas
The Glitter or The Gold – Suzanne Gilchrist
Christmas at the Cyprus Café – Susanne Bellamy
A Place to Belong – Annie Seaton
A Magical Summer - Rhonda Forrest

Destined to Stay – Kerrie Paterson
Home for Christmas – Lauren K McKellar
The Christmas Surprise – Linda Charles
The Gift of Bindarra Creek – Lindsay Douglas

A Bindarra Creek Christmas Romance
The Mistletoe Wish – Suzanne Gilchrist
The Christmas Jinx – Susanne Bellamy
The Grinch of Bindarra Creek – Lindsay Douglas
Christmas at Forrest Glen - Rhonda Forrest
Mistletoe Magic – Erin Moira O'Hara
Mistletoe and Blue Jeans – Linda Charles
A Clever Christmas – Annie Seaton
Tangled by Tinsel – Phillipa Nefri Clark
A Cowboy for Christmas – Lauren K McKellar

A Bindarra Creek Mystery Romance
A Dangerous Secret – Suzanne Gilchrist
Beyond the Gate – Rhonda Forrest
Protecting their Destiny – Erin Moira O'Hara
Only She Knew – Linda Charles
Secrets of River Cottage – Annie Seaton
Forgotten Secrets – Susanne Bellamy
A Perfect Danger – Phillipa Nefri Clark

Bindarra Creek A Town Reborn
Take Me Home – Suzanne Gilchrist
In the Heat of the Night – Susanne Bellamy
No Looking Back - Linda Charles

Worth the Wait – Annie Seaton
With Every Breath – Lauren K. McKellar
Stealing Her Heart – Simone Angela
A Twist of Fate – Erin Moira O'Hara
Promise Me Forever – Juanita Kees

Bindarra Creek Short & Sweet
What's in a Kiss – Linda Charles
My Forever Valentine – Sandie James
Pearls and Green Beer – Susanne Bellamy
Full Circle – Annie Seaton
Date with Destiny – Erin Moira O'Hara
A Letter From the Queen – Lee Christine
Love's Sweet Challenge – Suzanne Gilchrist
The Widow Maker – Lauren K. McKellar
Out of the Blue – Noelle Clark

Bindarra Creek Romance
Bindarra Creek Makeover – Suzanne Gilchrist
Shadows of the Heart - Lee Christine
Second Chance Love - Susanne Bellamy
The CEO Mechanic - Sandie James
Reach for the Stars - Kerrie Paterson
Home to Bindarra Creek - Juanita Kees
Stolen Sanctuary - Stacey Nash
Tempting Fate - Erin Moira O'Hara
One More Day - Linda Charles
The Vine - Lauren K. McKellar
The Ghost of His Past - Simone Angela

Joanie's Dilemma - Marianne Theresa
Buckley's Chance - Noelle Clark

Full details on buy links for all books in the Bindarra Creek world can be found at: www.bindarracreekromance.com

A glimpse into Billie & Kirk's story...

**The Glitter or The Gold - Copyright © 2023
Suzanne Gilchrist**

Humming along to the catchy song on the radio, Billie Miller scrubbed the area around the tiny hole in the car's exhaust pipe with a steel toothed brush. Once satisfied she'd eliminated the dirt and rust, she smoothed it off with a fine grit sandpaper. Tossing the sandpaper to one side, she took a moment to wipe beads of sweat from her forehead with the sleeve of her overalls. Although it was only late September, the tin shed she was working in thrummed with stifling heat. If this was a sign of the weather to come, she'd be wise to organise a swimming pool membership. Either that or spend the summer floating in the rockpool in Ward's Gully.

Which didn't sound like such a bad idea now that she came to think about it. Pausing, she imagined a picnic beneath shady willow trees with her elderly parents. A perfect memory to treasure; and a blessing if she could pull it off because the truth was, she didn't possess many happy family day memories. Not recent ones anyway; and that fault lay entirely on her shoulders and her obsession with building a successful mechanic business far from the small town of Bindarra Creek.

But that life was over, and here she was in her hometown living with her parents again at the ripe old age of thirty-nine - and counting.

She twitched her shoulders to push aside her unpleasant thoughts. Best not revisit the past or she'd never finish the job on hand. With a wiggle of her butt, she shifted the dolly-trolley she lay on under the old station wagon a tad to the right then groped for the bottle of acetone and a clean rag.

The song ended and immediately another Christmas tune took its place. The local station was seriously into the Christmas spirit even though there was still plenty of time before the holiday season began.

What would Christmas look like this year? Would her father even realise it *was* Christmas? Anguish gripped and twisted hard. Dementia was a real kick in the teeth for someone who had spent his entire life administering and helping others. *Life could be cruel.* But she had only herself to blame for staying away so long. At least, her father still recognised her. That was a blessing for which she was grateful for every day.

Flicking on her torch, she played the beam over the problem area. The small crack looked ready for the next step – applying the wet exhaust tape around the pipe. About to reach for the tape she paused as footsteps sounded over the hard concrete floor.

"Hello? Is anyone here?" called a pleasant male voice.

Her breathing hitched. She recognised that voice. Glaring at the undercarriage of the car, she willed her suddenly racing pulse to steady. That soft Yankee drawl had to belong to Kirk Wellington, given he was the only American in town. He'd arrived about four months ago, not that long after she had returned home. Apparently, he was an actor of all things and a relative of Ms Edwina Lette and her grandson, Dodge. Which unfortunately for Billie, meant too many encounters with him as her own mother and Ms Lette had always been tight as if an invisible bungee cord bound them together. Hence Billie had called her Auntie Edwina since she could talk. Even so, Billie had done her best to avoid him as much as possible on the occasions when she'd found herself in his company. He oozed sex appeal but it was more his engaging friendliness that disturbed her the most, triggering her hard-won defence system. She didn't need another relationship complication in her life – ever.

Which was a pity because he had the most tantalising smile and a way of holding her gaze as if she was someone truly special. With her hands motionless in the air, she stared blankly at the chassis above while she wasted a pleasant three whole seconds thinking about that smile until the sound of a throat clearing snapped her back to reality.

Annoyed with herself, she propelled out from under the car like a rocket, pushed to her feet and directed her scowl at the man who had recently begun to appear in her dreams. Not that she intended to admit it to anyone.

"Well?"

"Hi, there." His sparkling hazel eyes travelled over her dusty figure and his smile broadened into a grin. "I thought you might like to share lunch with me. Since it's my car you're working on."

"You're paying me. Or rather paying the garage owner," Billie said with a haughty sniff tacked on for good measure. "And no thanks, I'm not hungry."

Her stomach gave a traitorous growl.

Raising his eyebrows, Kirk waggled a large brown paper bag with grease stains in front of her face, giving her a good whiff of something seriously tasty. Was that a rissole and gravy sanga?

Her mouth watered.

"Courtesy of Warren's fabulous cooking. Do you know him?"

Billie shoved her hands into her pockets so she wouldn't be tempted to snatch the bag and wolf down the contents. "Of course, I do. He's Auntie's son-in-law or rather he was – before his first wife passed away."

"Mom told me how Cheryl died – snake bite – at Christmas time, if I remember correctly. That must have been devastating for everyone."

"Yeah, it was awful. I was maybe fifteen or sixteen at the time, and poor Dodge had just finished primary school. A terribly young age to lose your mother."

"Did you know her well?"

"Not so much. I only saw her at the shops or when I visited Auntie Edwina's place. I guess I was a typical teenager, self-absorbed back then; but I remember the funeral. Almost the entire town turned out to pay their respects. I remember thinking how shattered Warren and Auntie Edwina looked. Poor Dodge looked bewildered, as if he was stuck in some terrible dream."

"Or nightmare."

"Yeah." She looked away for a few beats, thinking back, about how the community, especially her parents, had rallied behind the bereaved family. About how kind people could be when needed. Feeling sad and a little guilty over how much she'd forgotten about her early life growing up in Bindarra Creek.

"Mom and dad left us kids with a nanny and flew over for a couple of days to give any support they could. Sad times, indeed. I can't image how Dylan must have felt. We're the same age, you know," said Kirk.

Lifting her chin, Billie gave him a tiny smile, trying to shift the sombre spell cast by past shadows. "Dodge, remember? Only Mrs Brown calls him Dylan. Not even his own dad."

"They seem close."

"They are that. Warren's a good bloke. He deserves to be happy and according to Mum, he is now thanks to Lou and the twins."

Kirk gave a theatrical shudder. "Those boys! Talk about energy! And the noise they make when they're chasing the dog around the house. Makes me exhausted listening to them." He grinned to show there was no malice behind his words. "Now, getting back to Warren and his divine cooking. I all but gallop down the stairs these days for breakfast and dinner. Which is playing havoc with my weight."

With a dramatic sigh, he patted his flat stomach. The faded blue jeans he wore hugged slim hips, firm thighs and long legs that ended above a pair of neon-green Nikes.

Billie's stare zeroed in on what was no doubt a six-pack stomach that rippled with muscles, hating the quivering deep in her belly. No sign of any excess weight that she could see. Had he done that on purpose? Directed her eyes to his body? Could he be teasing her? She already knew he liked to flirt. From what she'd seen, he seemed to direct his charm impartially onto anyone and everyone. She knew better than to believe he was seriously attracted to her especially since she was older than him by a few years. Now, if she was a young twenty-something year old, then matters might well be different. Not that *she* was interested of course.

"The food is getting cold." He opened the bag, releasing more of that aromatic scent.

Freshly baked bread. Rissoles. Gravy. Who could resist?

205

Buy Links can be found on the author's website: www.segilchrist.com

Acknowledgments

My special thanks to the wonderful critiquing skills and on-going motivation of authors, Ann B Harrison and Efthalia.

A shout out and thank you to Cindy Pearson for her awesome proofreading skills.

I'd also like to thank my fellow Bindarra Creek Christmas in July members for their enthusiasm for this series – it has been a joy working with you.

Last but never least, my sincere appreciation to my children for their wonderful support. And for continuing to cheer me on.

Acknowledgement of Country

In the spirit of reconciliation, the author and publisher acknowledges Aboriginal and Torres Strait Islander peoples as the First Australians and Traditional Custodians of the lands where we live, learn and work. We pay our respects to Elders past and present and all First Nations peoples and honour their unique cultural and spiritual relationships to the land, waters and seas and their rich contribution to society, and thank them for their ongoing custodianship of and care for Country.

About the Author

An Australian author, **S.E. Gilchrist**, combines romance with adventure and suspense across many genres including science fiction, apocalyptic, and contemporary small towns. Her sweet romances are written under **Suzanne Gilchrist**, and several of her books have been shortlisted in writing contests.

S.E. loves walking her two dogs, travelling, and spending time with family and friends. She co-runs the Hunter Romance Writers group and is the brainchild / organiser behind the multi-author, best-selling *Bindarra Creek Romance* series, as well as the *Mindalby Outback Romance* series and was a duo author in the *Deadly Forces* series.

She also participated in a multi-author collaboration under the writing name of J T Sloane in an 8-book post-apocalyptic survival thriller series called *'Swarm'* published by and with Mike Kraus.

Website: www.segilchrist.com